ESCAPE FROM
EAST BERLIN

ESCAPE FROM EAST BERLIN

ANDY MARINO

Scholastic Inc.

ISBN 978-1-338-83204-4

10 9 8 7 6 5 4 3 2 1   22 23 24 25 26

First edition, September 2022
Printed in the U.S.A.   40

Book design by Christopher Stengel

FOR NOAH

PROLOGUE

This wet suit is eight sizes too small," Johann Hoffmann says. He's slight and long-limbed, nicknamed *die Elritze*—the Minnow—by his fellow swimmers at the secondary school in Prenzlauer Berg, East Berlin. He reaches underneath his heavy peacoat and pulls at the rubber that hugs his body like a bandage.

"*Shhh,*" says his best friend, Stefan Dietrich. He keeps his voice near a whisper as the two boys creep through the shadows at the edge of the Alexanderufer, a road just east of Humboldt Harbor. "Why don't you yell at the *trapos* on the bridge and tell them we're coming?"

"Maybe I should," Johann says. "At least then it'll make things interesting."

Johann swims the anchor leg of the freestyle relay. He's the fastest swimmer on the team, but Stefan fears that his friend thinks he can outswim a bullet.

The blue-uniformed trapos—transit police—guard the new border between East and West Berlin, patrolling the sealed-off stations and train bridges that only three short months ago served as busy hubs for all Berliners. Every guard has been commanded to obey the order of *schiessbefehl*—the shoot-on-sight command issued from the very top of East Berlin's government.

There have been stories in the *Neues Deutschland* newspaper of border crossers losing their lives. Spies and agents of the Americans, the paper claims. Criminals, deserters, traitors. Weak-minded fools seduced by the West.

Stefan has pointed this out to Johann. Tried to get him to understand the danger of what they're about to do. But his friend only laughs.

They were trying to start a whole new life in the West. We're just crossing over for a few hours to visit Petra and Millie, then we're coming back home.

As if the trapos on the railway bridge can tell from a hundred meters away that a couple of idiots swimming the harbor at midnight are only going to West Berlin for a quick visit.

"That's us," Stefan mutters. "A couple of gigantic idiots."

"I wouldn't say *gigantic*," Johann says, only half as hushed as Stefan wishes he would be. "Maybe *regular* idiots?"

The Alexanderufer is a wide street with a concrete median splitting it in two. Stefan can see headlights approaching from a kilometer away. Then comes the telltale rattle of the engine of a Trabant—the boxy "spark plug on wheels" that's everywhere in East Berlin.

Without a word, the boys duck down behind a trash can. Stefan wrinkles his nose at the stench of rotten fruit.

Johann laughs softly as the Trabant clatters past. "Listen to that engine *purr*."

"Petra drives a Volkswagen," Stefan says wistfully. Before the wall went up on the night of August 13, East and West were divided by a million other things. If your family owned a reliable car that didn't sound like an accident waiting to happen, you probably lived in the West.

"I hope she's got some towels down when she picks us up," Johann says. "Or we'll get nasty harbor water all over those nice seats."

The Trabant chugs away south, turns along the horseshoe curve of the Spree, and vanishes into the night.

"Come on," Stefan says. Together, the boys move from behind the trash can and pick up the route along the street. Stefan's eyes roam the darkness. If they were to get stopped here, fifty meters from the harbor, dressed in winter coats and skintight wet suits, it would be a disaster.

He imagines the guard's astonishment at how easily he just caught a pair of obvious border crossers.

Cold night for a swim, boys.

Then they would be whisked away to the secret prison on the outskirts of East Berlin, the forbidden area he's only ever heard about in whispers.

"Stefan."

His mind reels with visions of isolation cells, maggots in the food, sleep deprivation . . .

That is, if they aren't simply shot on sight.

"Stefan!" Johann's voice pulls him back to reality.

Stefan's heart races. He takes a breath, tries to locate the sense of calm he always finds before he jumps off the blocks to lead their relay team. "What is it?"

"Did you bring any snacks?"

"We're about to jump into the harbor."

"Do you think Petra will have some?"

Suddenly, a searchlight blinks on like a flicked switch, from nothing to something.

"Get down!"

Stefan pulls his friend into the mulch that makes up a little strip of earth between the street and the harbor's edge. Together, they scramble behind a low-slung, makeshift lean-to—nothing more than a tarp stretched over some scrap wood, sheltering a pile of rusted pipes.

The light sweeps across the top of their hiding place. Stefan presses himself into the dirt.

"It's coming from up on the train bridge," he whispers.

The roving beam changes direction and pokes around the street, the empty dirt strip, the concrete embankment. The way it moves reminds Stefan of his Rottweiler puppy, Penelope, chasing squirrels in the Volkspark Friedrichshain. Darting this way and that, picking up one scent after another, overwhelmed by sensation. In this way, the beam is disturbingly alive. As it zips across the embankment, leaving them in darkness, Johann peeks above the tarp.

"I guess they're not using the train bridge for trains anymore," he says.

Cautiously, Stefan raises his head. An odor wafts up from the embankment: that fishy, briny smell he associates with the open sea, not a grubby little bottleneck of an inland harbor. The hulking shadow of a barge glides out from beneath the bridge. A man in a peaked cap floats by in a little square of light, a specter in the boat's wheelhouse. Stefan raises his eyes to the bridge. At first, he can't see much of anything with the searchlight blinding him. But as the beam slides away across the black water, his eyes adjust. There are men on the walkway between the tracks and the guardrail. A dozen of them, at least.

A cold knot forms in his gut. "Trapos. Tons of them."

"They weren't there yesterday," Johann says. They'd come by after school to scout their route. Unlike the other checkpoints, choked with razor wire and guards, the harbor seemed like an afterthought for the border patrol. Yesterday, they'd seen a total of two trapos. There was even a train line from the West that had to use the bridge to loop through the eastern section. The city had never been designed to be sliced in half overnight, so little quirks like this remained up and down the border. Bulges in the wall, as if the city's soft center were being squeezed out like clay in a fist.

"Maybe we should come back some other time," Stefan suggests.

"And by then, Petra and Millie will have lots of time to think about how stupidly hard it is to see us, and how easy it is to see the boys in West Berlin. They'll decide it's really not worth it, all this sneaking around and waiting in the dark for these two regular-idiot swimmers to climb out of Humboldt Harbor and get smelly dead-fish water all over the leather seats of their beautiful—"

"Okay, Johann—"

"—Volkswagen."

"—I get it."

"So off they go, Petra and Millie both, back to Charlottenburg for a couple of Coca-Colas in the American sector, where they just happen to run into two guys from their class. You know, the two best football players in all of West Berlin. *Very* handsome. Who also happen to have two empty seats at their table—"

"Johann!"

But Stefan knows this is plausible enough. And it isn't like they can rush home to call the girls and explain why they didn't show up. There haven't been telephone links between East and West Berlin since Stefan and Johann were eight years old. Now, at seventeen, the boys rely on the steadily dwindling workers who are still allowed to cross the border—under close supervision—to commute to their jobs. For the price of a few pfennigs, one of these commuters could be relied upon to pass messages to Millie and Petra. In this way, they make plans to meet—but such plans take days, or even weeks, to come together. Carrier pigeons would be a more efficient system. Messages in a bottle placed on the Spree, perhaps.

Cautiously, with just the top of his head poking above the tarp, Stefan rethinks their plan. The searchlight pokes into the shadows of the opposite embankment. Stefan watches, absorbing the layout of the western side of the harbor. As the light moves across the rickety wooden steps that rise from an old mooring jetty—the exit point they scouted yesterday—Stefan is struck by a feeling of profound unease. It's not fear, exactly, though there is a little of that too. It's more like the idea that the city itself is betraying them from within. That what they counted on as real, as solid as the pavement, can be changed overnight. Borders closed according to the wills of stern old politicians Stefan will never meet, and who will never know his name.

What will the city look like tomorrow morning, or the morning after that?

Who's to say those faceless politicians won't decide to wall in Prenzlauer Berg, or Kreuzberg, or Friedrichshain? Who would stop them?

The searchlight darts back across the harbor. It scans the water, then moves along the edges of the train bridge—the trapos aiming it straight down, so the beam is a vertical tower of light connecting harbor to bridge.

"We gonna sit here all night?" Johann says, rubbing his upper arms and shoulders. "It's freezing."

"The bridge," Stefan says, following the path of the searchlight. "Instead of going straight across and aiming for that old jetty, we cross directly underneath the bridge. The light can't find us there."

Johann takes off his jacket, bunches it up, and stashes it beneath the tarp with the pipes. He makes a fist and holds it up. Stefan lays a hand atop his friend's fist, palm to knuckles.

"What do we say to second place?" Johann asks.

"Nothing," Stefan answers. "Second place doesn't exist."

Their familiar pre-race chatter is a comfort. He feels a pang of longing for Jonas and Michael, the other two members of their freestyle relay. He invited them to come along tonight, but they declined. How amazing would *that* be, the four of them hitting the black water of Humboldt Harbor as one, the fastest relay team in East Berlin crossing right under the trapos' noses, there and back before dawn . . .

Ah, well. The other boys don't know what they're missing.

Stefan clears his mind and feels his body give over to his training. He enters a space where jitters and calm are perfectly in balance, alert but not overly keyed up. He removes his own jacket and stuffs it onto the pile next to Johann's. Then he takes off his shoes and hides them too. He blows hot air into his cupped hands, rubs his shoulders, and waits for the searchlight to drift toward the opposite embankment. A stray dog's mournful howl floats across the harbor. Stefan thinks of Penelope, then clears his mind.

With that, he leads Johann in a low jog across the dirt strip. The land dips sharply toward the water as the struts of the bridge rise from the earth. For a brief moment, the moonlight seems bright as the sun, and Stefan feels horribly exposed. One of the trapos laughs, and it sounds like he's right beside them. The two boys duck low to enter the triangular cavern formed by the slope of the embankment and the span of the bridge just above their heads. Here the smell of brine is laced with the sour odor of unwashed fabric and dirty clothing. They move past what appears to be an encampment of sorts. For a moment, Stefan is confused. In communist East Germany, there are not supposed to be any homeless people. Everyone has a job. The state makes sure of it.

The boots of the trapos clank on the bridge's flat span, just above their heads. At the water's edge is an old stone wall, one of those urban relics from the end of the Second World War, when Berlin was a bombed-out husk of itself. Here and there, the wall is pocked with holes and missing bricks. Stefan leads Johann down by feel, silently willing the opposite side to be just as friendly to midnight climbers. Moving carefully, he slides his bare feet along the slick, slimy stones until he finds a toehold. Then he inches his way down. They could jump, of course, and easily survive—the height of the embankment isn't the problem. It's the noise of the splash he's worried about.

His toe dips into the water. The cold zaps his entire body. What feels like an electric current buzzes through his teeth. He takes a breath and drops in. The wet suit lessens the shock, but it's not a magic cloak. They have to get moving before their limbs go numb.

"Not so bad," Johann whispers, bobbing next to him in the black water. But Stefan can hear the strain in his friend's voice. "Tropical. Bathwater. Anyway. Race you to the other side."

As Johann stretches out into a quick yet careful forward crawl, Stefan matches his strokes. Despite the incredible, breathtaking cold, Stefan feels a slight tug of satisfaction pulling him smoothly onward. He lets his mind flash to the upcoming 1964 Olympics in Tokyo. His nerves are distant, chattering at the edge of his mind, easily ignored. An openhearted feeling washes over him. He'd always thought Johann would surely make the team, but why should he have to settle for a spectator's role? If he keeps training hard, there's no reason they can't keep the relay team together, all the way to the international stage, swimming against the best in the world. As he knifes through the freezing harbor, sheltered by the train bridge, he imagines the rush of the water as the roar of a crowd.

With the sensitivity of a sea creature, Stefan notes a sudden absence in the water at his side. Die Elritze has pulled ahead, outpacing him as they near the halfway point. Stefan changes his strokes carefully—unlike in a race, when he can focus all his energy toward that forward motion no matter how noisy it gets, he has to maintain a smooth, even stroke. His lightly cupped hands drag water like oars, propelling him onward. He feels the pleasant strain on the muscles of his upper back. The rhythmic quarter turns of his head provide quick glimpses of the strange aquatic cavern he finds himself in. So dark, so cold. His Olympic daydream creeps around the edges of his mind, poking and prodding as he pursues his friend. The crowd roars. The cameras flash.

Wait.

The cameras flash?

He comes to a dead stop in the water as his brain beats back the fantasy and reality pours in.

A second searchlight pierces the night. Smaller than the first, dialed down to a precise beam that cuts through the darkness beneath the bridge. Stefan swivels his neck to the source. A small boat, idling in the water, ten meters away. A light is mounted on its bow, pinning Johann in the water.

Die Elritze's face is twisted into a grimace as he stares into the brightness. Stefan's mind spins out—Johann can't see a thing, but Stefan can, and what he sees is a pair of trapos flanking the mounted searchlight and raising their rifles. They yell for Johann to *STOP*, which strikes him as absurd because Johann is already frozen in place.

Stefan realizes that they don't know he's here. And even if they do, they can't possibly see him if he stays well outside the scope of their searchlight. He could dive right now, swim through the depths until his lungs are set to burst, and come up for air far from the boat. He could climb out, retrieve his jacket and shoes, vanish into the night . . .

His arms go up. His arms go down. He splashes.

"Hey!" His voice rings out. Without a plan, without a *thought*, he flails and yells. "Over here!"

The beam leaves Johann in the dark and zips across the water. A moment later, Stefan is blinded. Bright light is all around him.

"Johann!" he screams. "Go!"

"Not without you!" his friend calls back.

There are orders being shouted from the boat by men he can't see. *Be quiet* and *swim toward us slowly*. Stefan ignores them.

"I'll see you in Tokyo!" he calls out to Johann.

Then he plunges into the sightless depths. His body goes vertical—head down, feet up. He aims straight for the bottom.

There's a sound like a distant hammer, a short, sharp strike of a nail into a wall. At the same time, the hammer strikes his leg, just above his right knee. His body does a somersault. The darkness is so pure, up and down are jumbled. His leg goes numb and also heavy with a dull yet immense pain that seems to weigh him down. He has a wild flash of memory: a book about surviving an avalanche. The first thing you're supposed to do when you've come to a stop inside an enormous mound of snow is spit. You can always tell which way is up by the way your spit falls. But how is he supposed to do that in water? There is no gravity here.

He commands his body to right itself. He commands his legs to kick, his arms to pull against a million billion tons of water flowing into the river Spree. There's another muffled, distant *crack*, and it's like someone slammed a huge piece of burning steel into his rib cage. It's wormed its way into his body, crowding out his lungs, weighing him down like an anchor. He must not have taken in enough air. Yes, that's it: He only has to swim to the surface, poke his head up, gulp some sweet oxygen. But he's spinning through the darkness, and it's so much colder down here now. How deep is Humboldt Harbor, anyway? Then it hits him, and he nearly laughs despite this weird dizzy feeling that makes it hard to hold on to a thought for very long.

The light!

He only has to swim toward the searchlight! That's his version of spitting in the snow. Sure, the men with their guns will be waiting for him, but he needs air. At least on the surface he'll have a chance. He aims his body toward the distant pool of light. For a moment, nothing happens. Then, as he tries to put together a kick—which doesn't work because his body's like a stopped clock—the searchlight widens and grows and comes down toward him, seeking him, angling itself through the depths as it fills the harbor with light. When that vast beam reaches him, he finds that he's no longer cold.

There's another *crack*—this one impossibly distant, like it's coming from the world outside his window as he sleeps, echoing through a winter dream. Something tugs at the back of his neck, near the base of his spine, but it doesn't pull him down. It lifts him up, up, up through the radiant light. He doesn't even need to kick his legs or move his arms. It's like when the swim team does backstroke drills in practice and he propels himself with the lane divider for a little added momentum when Coach isn't looking. Everybody does it. Even die Elritze. It's just a little private joke among the team.

And then—the strangest thing.

He is swimming again, outside the water, rising through the night air. There are the trapos on the bridge, excited and chattering and milling about like ants in a colony, pointing down into the water, peering over the rail's edge. But it's hard to spare them a moment's thought, because all his senses have come screaming back now that he's out of the murky depths. All around him, Berlin sparkles. The stately columns of the Brandenburg Gate, the palace of Charlottenburg, the blinking lights of the tower at Tempelhof Airport—and due east, his apartment block in Prenzlauer Berg, where his parents and his sister, Marta, and Penelope the Rottweiler sleep without the faintest idea that he has snuck out to swim across the border.

He finds that it's hard to spare even *them* a moment's thought, because as he rides the jet stream up through the clouds, he's a radio antenna for the divided city as it sleeps.

Or tries to.

Thousands of citizens toss and turn, kept awake by thoughts of this new wall that splits their beloved Berlin in two. The city, pregnant with decades of conflict, has birthed an abomination.

It began with the war, thinks an old woman in Spandau, pulling her woolen blankets up to her chin.

No—thinks a man in Kreuzberg, where the barbed wire has split the street in two—*it began with the other war, the earlier one, which in its horrors paved the way for the second.*

Another insomniac voice joins the chorus that floats above the city: *You're both wrong. It's the fault of the decadent Westerners, the Americans and the British and the French. If it weren't for their violent imperialist ways, we wouldn't need the Anti-Fascist Protection Barrier in the first place.*

You fool, adds a voice from Neukölln. *What kind of sick government needs a wall to keep its citizens* in? *That's communism for you. No wonder everyone in the East wants to escape to the West.*

Stefan's last thought before it all becomes mist is this: *It's strange how everyone is fixated on the stupid wall, when from up here there's only one Berlin. No East, no West, no Anti-Fascist Protection Barrier—just one country, one city, one people.*

It is the right of every nation to protect its borders. What do the Western nations use to protect theirs? Friendly maidens who confront illegal border crossers with empty hands and apologetic smiles? Perhaps a single line painted on the ground, and a sign urging politely, Please Do Not Cross Here? Is Great Britain in the business of allowing all manner of foreign agents to cross back and forth with nothing but a stern warning not to misbehave? Do the French and the Americans allow anyone to sail to their shores or land in their airports without passing through a checkpoint?

Let us not mince words: There will be the usual moral scolding and hand-wringing judgment passed down from the anti-socialist elements. We all must disregard the empty words of hypocrites and forge ahead. Before the smears and lies come shrieking in from the West, we present you, the people of our glorious Workers' and Peasants' Republic, with the simple facts.

Last night, two young men we have long suspected of spying for the West attempted to cross our border. Their purpose was to hand over information to be used in violent acts of sabotage against the people of the German Democratic Republic. Our brave border guards were forced to use their weapons to prevent this illegal crossing and the mayhem that would surely follow. In the process, one of the spies, Johann Hoffmann, was taken into custody. His partner in crimes against the state, Stefan Dietrich, attempted to break free, endangering the lives of our border guards and nearby citizens. Left with no recourse, and concerned above all with public safety, these men were forced to do their duty.

Stefan Dietrich thereby died.

In the coming days, the West will try to paint this criminal as a hero. Make no mistake: He died as he lived.

An enemy of the German people.

CHAPTER

1

DECEMBER 9, 1961

There's been another one."

Marta Dietrich's father sets his Saturday edition of *Neues Deutschland* down on the kitchen table. The apartment goes silent. Marta pauses with a forkful of sliced banana—a rare breakfast treat—halfway to her mouth. Her mother rests a hand on her mug full of *Rostfein*, the coffee that hovers at around 50 percent genuine beans. Nobody moves. Then, slowly, her mother lowers her magazine. Marta's eyes flick to the cover, where a blond model is smiling like the world has just opened up its arms to greet her, over the words *New Styles for Winter.*

Marta glances at her father's hands as he folds them atop the newspaper and bows his head. Scattered words jump out from the page, peeking out from around his wrists—*criminal, spy, guards, duty, East, West, Americans.*

It might as well be that same dreadful article about her brother, Stefan, with the words rearranged. All these *Neues Deutschland* articles about border crossers tell the same story: an evil spy getting the justice he deserves.

The SED—the East German Communist Party—arranges reality the way they see fit. Marta saw the newspaper *Der Spiegel*, published in the West, before the wall went up. That paper sounds like someone laying out basic facts. *Neues Deutschland* sounds like someone desperate to prove a point.

Marta eats banana slices. Her mother sips coffee.

Her father gets up from the table. He goes to a small chalkboard on the wall and adds a line to the ten tally marks he's already made. He presses the chalk so hard, Marta's afraid it will break. Her father stands there, silently contemplating the tally.

"Eleven," he says.

Eleven East Germans killed trying to cross the border since the wall went up on August 13.

Her brother, Stefan, was number eight.

Marta's eyes go to the eighth tally mark. It looks the same as the rest, a white line on a chalkboard. All that's left of her older brother.

Above the tally is a basic grocery list: milk, butter, eggs, potatoes. The list never changes. It's only there to provide cover for the tally, should their apartment be visited by an agent of the Ministry for State Security. The secret police.

The Stasi.

They have paid Marta's family a visit on four separate occasions since Stefan's death. To the Stasi, the Dietrichs have two massive red flags in their file: Stefan's border-crossing attempt, and Marta's mother's former job in West Germany. Anyone who worked in the West before the wall went up is now viewed with suspicion.

Her father puts down the piece of chalk and wanders over to the toaster.

He lays a finger on the spring-loaded switch and presses it down. It pops back up. There's no bread in the toaster. It's not even plugged in. He peers into the empty slots, mutters to himself, then turns to the frost-rimed window. He rolls up his left sleeve, then unrolls it and lets it dangle from his forearm, loose and unbuttoned.

Marta slides the newspaper over to her side of the table and spins it so she can read the article.

"Marta," her mother says. But the warning is halfhearted. The argument could be scripted at this point, they've had it so many times.

"I'm twelve, Mutti. Not seven."

"You're twelve, Marta. Not seventeen."

Seventeen. Stefan's age. As old as he'll ever be.

Marta stabs another stack of banana slices and runs her eyes down the article. She's not really sure what her mother is trying to protect her from. The worst possible thing has already happened.

The scene described in the article paints itself into her mind: A railway goods station, the small hours of the morning. Wisps of fog, flickering streetlights. A wild-eyed man in his twenties, kneeling in a frigid puddle, trying to pry open a hastily made barrier that divides the train tracks. When spotted by the heroic border guards, he attempted to flee back into the East, from where he'd come.

The guards pursued him through the streets and shot him anyway, a few blocks from his home.

The point is clear: Even if you turn back, even if you have second thoughts, we will use lethal force to punish you.

What had they called Stefan? *An enemy of the German people.*

Marta taps a finger against the poorly printed text—some letters are gray, some smudged nearly to black. "They call this guy a 'leech sucking the blood of our healthy body.'"

She imagines a slimy, man-sized grub, writhing and slurping at the heart of East Germany itself, sinking his teeth into the pavement of Unter den Linden.

"It's a metaphor," her mother explains. Until August, Alma Dietrich had been a literature teacher in a secondary school in the Moabit neighborhood of West Berlin. She had been one of the thousands of East Berliners whose work took them on a daily commute over the border in the morning, and back home to the East in the evenings.

Now there is no more work in the West for residents of the East.

The education system here has no place for someone accustomed to teaching students Western values. Alma Dietrich has been reassigned by the labor exchange to a washing machine factory.

"Do you know the meaning of the term?" Marta's mother asks. "Metaphor?"

"I'm not sure if they teach creative thinking here in the East," her father mutters. His back is to the table. He takes one step closer to the window, tilts his forehead against the cold glass, and worries at the buttons of his cuffs. The windowpane rattles as he fusses.

"I know what a metaphor is," Marta says. "It's, like, a thing that doesn't exist used to describe something that *does* exist."

"Acceptable," her mother says.

"I still don't get how this man who tried to cross the border was sucking blood from the East, even if it is supposed to be a metaphor. Wasn't he just trying to leave?"

"To the Party," her mother explains, "we are the blood of East Germany. The citizens. We are the workers, after all, and workers are the engine of everything. Thus, everyone who leaves is another trickle of blood that weakens the body of the state. The wall was supposed to be the bandage to stop the bleeding, but instead it's becoming a wound—a great slice through the city itself, a gash in the fabric of the East." She nods at the chalkboard. "And it's getting infected."

Marta imagines the wall as an oozing sore. People from the East move like the blood cells she's seen in grainy filmstrips, and the wall bulges and shivers and gets redder and redder until—

"You're going to be late," her father says, pointing to the clock on the wall next to the chalkboard. The hands tick around a brightly colored picture of Riga, the Latvian coastal city where they vacationed last summer. Stefan and Marta had spent entire days in the sea, letting the waves knock them down, tumbling underwater, racing from the coastline to the little food stand at the north end of the beach—the hut shaped like a giant bratwurst. "You wouldn't want to miss a second of your highly educational field trip to"—he turns to Marta—"what is it today, the sock factory?"

"Um . . ." Marta closes one eye while she thinks of what Frau Vandenburg tried to get them excited about this week. "Manhole covers."

Her father shakes his head. His face is blank, weary—there's no mischief in his eyes anymore. "The manhole cover factory. Of course."

Every week, her school takes students on a trip to a factory or a collective farm. Today, she can look forward to spending her Saturday working alongside the employees at the manhole cover factory on the outskirts of the Hellersdorf district.

If the work is too dangerous or specialized for a bunch of kids, her class will help put together boxes for storage and shipping. If they're really lucky, they'll help file some old paperwork in the musty basement office.

"Maybe someday you'll come to visit Modern Washing Units," her mother says, nudging her shoulder, "and I can give you a biiiiiig hug in front of all your friends."

"Mutti!" Marta slides her chair away.

"And smother you in kisses! Oh, my sweet daughter, come see your loving mother! I'll come running across the factory floor to sweep you up!"

She purses her lips and leans in.

"Eww!" Marta turns her head.

Her father clears his throat. "Go get ready," he says. Marta meets his eyes. These days, when she looks at her father, he seems to be a copy of a copy of himself. He spends so much time moping around the apartment, staring at familiar, everyday objects as if they hold the key to releasing whatever pain he's hiding.

He turns back to the empty toaster. His finger hovers above the switch. He doesn't move.

Marta scarfs the last of the banana slices and excuses herself. She pauses at the living room window and looks out onto Bernauer Strasse, the wide street outside their building. She has peered out every day since August 13, and still the sight of the new wall astonishes her. An endless unfurling of razor wire and steel, buttressed with concrete tank traps like massive spiky knucklebones called "dragon's teeth," slicing her street in half.

There's a soft nuzzling against her leg. She bends over and scoops up Penelope, their Rottweiler puppy. It's technically her brother's dog—he was the one who brought her home, unannounced, one Sunday afternoon. In typical Stefan fashion, he'd simply walked in with her, along with a soft doggy bed and a bag of kibble, as if it were something the whole family had been planning for weeks. But nobody had objected.

"How could they say no to you?" Marta says, lifting the squirming pup. Penelope smothers her face with slobbery kisses. Marta loves how her brown and black patches are carefully arranged. She's not speckled like a Dalmatian; she's *composed* like a painting.

The phone rings. Penelope barks. Her little eyes dart back and forth and settle on Marta's face, eager for the comfort of a familiar sight.

Marta sets her down and the dog wanders back over to the bed, a fuzzy lump of gray fabric. Her mother's voice drifts in from the kitchen. A few curt phrases, a word or two, and then a goodbye. Penelope turns in a circle, becomes moderately interested in her tail, then plops down and licks a paw. Marta hears the phone click back into its receiver.

Her mother pops into the living room.

"That was Frau Vandenburg," she says. "There's been a fire at the manhole cover factory."

"That's great!" Marta says. "I mean, was anyone hurt?"

"No. It happened overnight. Marta, there are easier ways to get out of a boring field trip."

"I didn't do it!"

Her mother sighs. "I just hope you didn't leave any fingerprints."

"Mutti!"

Her father walks out of the kitchen. Marta glances at him, waiting for him to chime in with *This is a very serious matter, think of the manholes* before breaking into a grin, then contagious laughter. But instead he heads for the bedroom without a word and shuts the door. Marta watches her mother gaze after him. She half expects her father to open the door and announce that he was just kidding, that he couldn't possibly spend a Saturday locked away in his bedroom, but there is only quiet stillness. She gives it another few seconds, hoping that her father—the one she's always known, not this strange new one—will emerge. Nothing happens.

"Well," Marta says to break the silence, "I guess I've got a free Saturday for once."

She plops down on the sofa, puts her feet up on the coffee table, and picks up an old issue of *Sibylle* magazine.

"Lucky you," her mother says. "Now you can bring some leftover pork schnitzel to your cousin Harry and the kids."

"Okay," Marta says, turning the page, pretending to read. Penelope hops up next to her and nudges the magazine with her nose.

"And you can bring it over *now*, so they can have it for lunch."

"I've really been looking forward to catching up on this magazine."

"Marta."

As if she's been zapped into slow motion, Marta sets the magazine down and gets robotically to her feet.

Her mother disappears into the kitchen and emerges a moment later with a casserole dish covered in tinfoil.

Behind the closed door, the springs of her parents' mattress creak. Her father has gone back to bed.

utside, Marta balances the casserole dish on her forearm like a waitress. She pulls up her knit scarf to cover her face. The scarf had been Stefan's. It's as white as the dusting of snow that covers the streets like spilled sugar—the color of Dynamo Berlin, her brother's favorite football team. Marta thinks of it as winter camouflage, imagines it wrapping all around her like a magic cloak.

It's very cold today. Her breath puffs out from the scarf's loose knit.

Standing at the bottom of her building's small front stoop, she gazes across the street. There's the wall, more formidable out here than it appears from their window four floors up. She turns her head to the left, then to the right—the barrier runs down the center of the grand avenue as far as she can see.

A wound.

A gash in the fabric of the city.

Every ten meters, a giant metal uppercase Y juts up from the concrete like some awful flower. Each Y is taller than her father, taller even than Stefan's swim coach, who is practically twice her height. Curls of barbed wire connect the bottom halves of each Y. The top half is strung with lengths of straight wire, making it impossible to scale the barrier with a ladder. If she were to stand right next to the curly wire and look up, there would be the straight wire above her head. And if anyone tries to crash through the wire with their Trabant, well—that's what the rows of dragon's teeth are for.

"Marta! *Guten morgen!*" Herr Schmidt, a neighbor from the third floor, bustles past her up the steps with a grocery bag. His plump, ruddy face is wrapped in a checked scarf and brown hat. "Tell your mother to get down to the Konsum!" The man is nearly out of breath. He fumbles for his keys. "They have bananas for once—and they're going fast!"

"I had a delicious banana this morning, thank you," Marta says.

"One step ahead of everyone, as usual." Herr Schmidt pushes open the door and nearly fumbles the bag. He lowers his voice. "The Stasi can't hold a candle to Alma Dietrich."

Marta blinks. Was that a threat? An accusation? Or a harmless joke?

Any mention of the secret police in public is like a dark spell—it gives her goose bumps and fouls the air. She tries to smile politely. Herr Schmidt disappears into the building without another word.

It's probably just Herr Schmidt's version of the *Berliner Schnauze*, that famously impolite sense of humor some city dwellers are famous for.

"Okay," she says out loud. Since Stefan died, she has divided up her day into little chunks of time. Her mother says everyone grieves differently. But Marta thinks her brain might be malfunctioning.

"Okay," she says again. She imagines the word like scissors, cutting the minutes up into little fragments. She can stand here on the front porch and watch her neighborhood come to life (okay) and the wall rise from the street (okay) and Herr Schmidt push past her with his bag of bananas from the

Konsum (okay), and each little snippet of time is time without her brother. But she can get through each day as long as it doesn't stretch out endlessly. (Like she suspects it does for her father.)

As long as it's snipped into bite-sized pieces, she only has to get to the next *okay*.

Before she heads to her cousin Harry's, she peers intently through the wire. Directly across the divided street is a gorgeous old apartment block. Some of its bricks are shinier, newer, less weathered than others—a jigsaw puzzle put back together after the Allied bombing of the 1940s. Marta's eyes land on the third window from the left, two floors down from the top.

A dim figure behind parted curtains lifts a hand and waves. Marta waves back.

"Hi, Markus," she says, hoping maybe her cousin can read her lips.

She has grown up with Markus and the rest of her extended family. They were all neighbors for as long as Marta could remember. And then she woke up on the morning of August 13 to find that Cousin Markus and his family now lived in the West while Cousin Harry and his family lived in the East. The story is the same for families up and down Bernauer Strasse. A close-knit neighborhood split in two. Friends they'd known since childhood out of reach.

The cruelty of this seems deliberate to Marta.

She makes a sour fish-face at Markus, then flips it into a smile before heading northeast on Bernauer Strasse, toward the Mauerpark. It's the same route she'd take to school. She reminds herself how fortunate she is to have a free Saturday—as rare as the bananas in the Konsum supermarket—and moves quickly along the sidewalk through the brisk morning air. The streets aren't crowded. Since the wall went up in August, there's been a sense of emptiness gripping her neighborhood.

Harry's building is across from the Mauerpark, where the wall cuts due north along the edge of the greenery. Here the border looks like a true frontier, with the wire fence dividing the city in the West and the wilderness in the East.

The front door to the building is open. A stocky man is leaning against the doorjamb with one leg bent, looking very relaxed. A candy cane juts from his mouth, its shepherd's crook shiny and crystalline. Unkempt straw-colored hair frizzes out from beneath a shapeless black cap. Mirrored aviator sunglasses hide his eyes. He looks like photographs she's seen of Western poets gathering in a café. There had been a presentation in school by some government official about the ridiculous youth culture of the West. It was supposed to have been an example of how the capitalists would destroy themselves from within. And now, standing in the doorway to Cousin Harry's building, is someone who looks as if he leapt out of that filmstrip.

Marta nearly bursts out laughing as he takes the candy cane from his mouth and whistles, slightly off-key. The melody is familiar. The lyrics run through her mind.

He sees you when you're sleeping . . .

The man brushes past Marta without acknowledgment, tosses the candy cane into the gutter, and heads down the street, still whistling.

He knows when you're awake . . .

Marta watches him saunter away with a grinding of gears in the back of her mind. There's something familiar about the man, but she can't put her finger on it. He turns a corner and disappears. "Okay," she says. She doesn't even have to buzz Harry's flat to be let in. The candy-cane man left the door open.

Noise leaks into the hallway, a din like the Republic Day parade has been stuffed into a tiny apartment. Marta stands outside the door to her cousin's flat and closes her eyes, listening.

A baby cries.

A toddler shrieks.

Pots and pans clatter.

A third child yells *MUTTI!*

A Rundfunk der DDR radio broadcast reports on the latest escape attempt.

Her cousin's busy household is in a constant state of near catastrophe. She relishes it, lets the voices wash over her. How different it is from the sleepy underwater mood of her own apartment. She thinks of the mattress creaking as her father headed back to bed. He used to do laps at the *schwimmhalle* every Saturday morning, the same crisp freestyle stroke his son, Stefan, would perfect as he knifed through the water. Now she wonders if her father will ever swim again. The sight of water seems to make him ill-tempered and depressed.

Words from the radio broadcast float into the hall. *Traitor* and *spy* and *fascist agent*.

Okay.

Marta opens her eyes and raps her knuckles against the door. Five hard knocks.

A moment later it swings open. Harry's wife, Monika, moving like a whip, snaps into place on the other side. Her apron is dusted with flour. There's a smear of batter on her forehead. She clutches a toy fire engine and a mixing bowl to her chest.

Her face is scrunched in annoyance. Then she sees her visitor and a smile breaks out.

"Marta! What a nice surprise. Welcome to the zoo. You're just in time for the first feeding of the day. We're running a little behind schedule this morning." She leans back and glances off to the side. "Hans!" she calls out. "Don't climb on that!" She turns to Marta and exhales deeply. "The animals are restless." A little girl toddles over and twines her arms around Monika's leg. She stares curiously up at Marta. Monika brightens. "Cute, though. Come in, come in."

Marta steps inside her cousin's flat. Monika nudges the door closed with her foot. The toddler clings.

Marta smiles at the scrawny little girl. "Good morning, Ingrid."

Ingrid stares back, unblinking, then hides her eyes behind her mother's leg.

Marta takes in the interior. The place is about half the size of her apartment up the street and twice as crowded. The coffee table is piled with toys that spill off the edge to scatter across the carpet. In this messy nest sits the youngest child, Joachim, cross-legged in his cloth diaper and snap-button top. He crashes two brightly colored building blocks together and makes spluttery engine noises.

"Hans!" Monika says again. She crosses the living room, lifting Ingrid along with her leg. "Down! Now!"

The second youngest, a shirtless boy of six, reluctantly stops dancing and hops down off the kitchen table. Then he puts his arms out to imitate the wings of a plane and dive-bombs his way through the living room.

"Hi, Marta," says the oldest boy, ten-year-old Gerhard, lying on the sofa. His head is inches from the radio on the end table. "Somebody tried to crash a truck through the border in Pankow."

"I heard," Marta says.

Gerhard's face betrays no emotion. He stares up at a brown water stain on the ceiling.

"Gerhard," Monika says as she plunks the mixing bowl down on the table, "for the last time, turn the radio off and go to school, please."

"They shot him nine times," Gerhard says, ignoring his mother. "Right through the windshield."

"Gerhard!" Monika says.

Gerhard's eyes meet hers and Marta doesn't blink. "I heard," she says again.

Gerhard reaches behind his head and turns the dial without looking. The stern broadcast voice goes silent. Hans strafes Joachim's position on the carpet, buzzing past and snatching the block out of his hand. Joachim bursts into shrieking hysterics.

"Go. To. School!" Monika says.

Gerhard pushes himself up with a sigh and heads for the bedroom he shares with his siblings. He pauses halfway and glowers at Marta. "Why aren't *you* in school today?"

"Fire at the manhole cover factory. Trip got canceled."

He shakes his head. "Agents from the West, sabotaging our industry."

"Who knows," Marta says. Then she goes to the kitchen and sets the casserole dish down on the table. Monika swirls a whisk around the mixing bowl. Ingrid lets go of her mother's leg and crawls beneath the table. Joachim wails a single drawn-out note. Monika curses under her breath.

"Pork schnitzel," Marta announces, "from my mother."

"Ach," Monika says, "bless her. Hans!" she calls to the six-year-old, who is now making loud *bbbrrrrapppp* noises as he spirals around his shrieking little brother. "Turn on the Piko!" Underneath the table, Ingrid plays a drumbeat against Marta's toes. Hans zooms off to the corner of the living room, by the television.

A mechanical whirring sound fills the room. Instantly, Joachim quiets down. Marta turns to watch. A shiny red model locomotive comes chugging out from behind the television, trailing a long row of multicolored boxcars. The toy track has been expertly laid along a small shelf that juts out like a drawbridge from the credenza holding the television. From there, the train dips, vanishes, and emerges a moment later from underneath the sofa, to complete a loop of rolling hills that takes it past the one window looking out upon Bernauer Strasse and back to the station by the television.

"Speaking of trains," Marta says, "where's Harry?"

Gerhard emerges from the bedroom, knapsack slung over a shoulder. Monika gives Marta a look she can't read, then smiles at Gerhard. "Have a nice day at school."

"Bye," he says, and leaves the apartment.

Monika waits a moment, her eyes moving slowly along the wall, as if she can see into the hallway beyond and watch Gerhard walk away. "Your cousin's out back," she says.

The model train blows its whistle. Joachim claps in delight and rolls onto his back. Hans jumps up and begins to dance on the couch. Ingrid crawls out from under the table and opens the cupboard beneath the sink. Then she slams it shut. Then she opens it again.

"Tell him we're in desperate need of a zookeeper, please."

Marta crosses the living room, weaves through a landscape of fallen blocks, stoops to pat Joachim on the head, and opens a narrow door.

"Marta, watch this!" Hans calls out. She turns. The boy performs a surprisingly good jump kick, then lands on his back on the couch and bounces to his feet.

"Amazing!" She gives him a little wave, then goes through the door into a between place that brings to mind an airlock from one of Stefan's science-fiction novels. A vivid image flashes in her mind—her brother's room, exactly as he left it on his last night alive, lurid paperbacks scattered across his messy floor. Twig-thin aliens and orange moons and people in bulky space suits.

Her parents haven't touched a thing. A museum to Stefan's life.

Okay.

Marta moves through a narrow, dimly lit hallway until she comes to another door. Its gray paint is chipped and peeling, like the door at her school marked BOILER ROOM.

She stops and listens to the voices on the other side. Two men. One, her cousin Harry, excitable and jabbering. She places an ear to the cool metal door. The hum of the building's furnace vibrates inside her head as she eavesdrops.

"You know as well as I do," Harry says, "they haven't sealed off all the ghost stations yet. All we have to do is divert the tracks!"

"For the hundredth time, Dietrich!" The second man's voice is like a mouthful of chewed gravel. "We're DR operators. The ghost stations are U-Bahn. We're better off using the long-haul routes, finding a weakness in the border that way."

"There's no time," Harry insists. "Every day there's a new fence, another checkpoint. It's a different world underground. I'm telling you, I've seen the ghost stations with my own eyes!"

Marta knows that the DR—the Deutsche Reichsbahn—is the long-haul railway that takes East Germans from city to city, connecting Hamburg with Berlin and Frankfurt and Dresden. Not to be confused with the S-Bahn and U-Bahn trains, which whisk commuters from station to station inside Berlin.

But what are the ghost stations?

And why are they looking for a weakness in the border? Is her cousin going to try to escape to the West?

"Your haste is going to get us killed," the second man says. "Look what they did to your own cousin!"

Harry's voice comes back low and fierce. "You know as well as I do that Stefan was betrayed. It wasn't just a lucky shot from a trapo. They were waiting for him under that bridge."

Marta's heart begins to race. Dizzy thoughts swirl around the single ugly word: *betrayed*. Her brother, ratted out by an informer. Some busybody like Herr Schmidt using Stefan's life to score a few cheap points with the Stasi. She crushes her ear harder against the door, waiting for the dull pain to blot out the word. But the idea behind it is too vast to ignore: a city full of people who aren't what they seem. And somehow, the weight of all these sad little secrets came down on Stefan, dragging him into the depths of Humboldt Harbor. It isn't fair.

Now her cousin is going to take the same stupid risk. She imagines her father making chalk line number twelve for Harry. Before she knows what she's doing, she shoves open the metal door.

"You can't go!" she blurts out.

Suddenly, a pair of strong arms seize her roughly by the shoulders and a strange man's face is all she can see. His hair is bristly and short. A black patch covers his left eye.

"Quiet, child!" he snarls. "What have you heard?"

It's all right!" Harry darts into view and pulls the man back. "It's just my cousin." Marta rubs the feeling back into her upper arms. The stranger who seized her is hulking and broad shouldered, wearing soot-stained denim overalls. He scowls at Harry, then moves his one-eyed gaze to Marta with great suspicion.

The big man shrugs Harry off and flicks a hand down the front of his overalls.

"You can't just jump out at people like that," Harry tells him. "We've been over this."

They are all three standing in a space no bigger than a closet, an air shaft open to the sky. Beneath her feet is a metal grate above the furnace that heats the building, fed by a metallic octopus of pipes that vanish into the darkness.

It never fails to make her laugh that Harry and Monika call this place "out back," as if it were a lovely patio.

"The girl surprised me is all," the big man mutters. He runs a hand across the top of his buzzed head.

Harry clears his throat. As usual, he's wearing a plaid checked jacket one size too big. It defies any kind of fashion Marta is aware of, Eastern or Western. His dark hair is unruly, but in a precise way, like a famous person pretending to be caught unaware for a magazine photographer. As he leans back against the brick wall, he gives off the attitude of a musician in a night-club taking a break.

He is surely the oddest train engineer in all of East Berlin.

"Marta," he says, beckoning her closer, as if there were any great distance to cross. He gestures to the man at his side. "This is Helmut, the fireman on locomotive 519."

Helmut shifts his weight from one foot to the other and folds his arms across his massive chest.

"Helmut's jokes are legendary," Harry says, grinning broadly, as if the two men are on a stage. "Tell my cousin the one about the wood chipper, the foot-ball, and the blue jay." Helmut's good eye narrows. He doesn't speak. "Maybe some other time, then. Now, Marta! What brings you to this end of Bernauer Strasse?" He pauses. "Wait—what's today? Saturday, isn't it?" He fixes Marta with a mischievous look.

Marta guesses her cousin's question before he can ask it. "There was a fire at the manhole cover factory."

Helmut snorts.

"You know, Marta," Harry says, "when I was a boy we pretended to be *sick* to get out of school. Setting a fire is a bit extreme, don't you think?" He sighs. Marta smiles—*already heard that one today, Harry.* "But I suppose we can't deny the effectiveness." He elbows the man at his side. "Helmut here knows a thing or two about fires. Isn't that right?"

Helmut grunts. "How many cousins do you *have*, Dietrich?"

"Forty-six!" Harry says. "Of which thirty-four now find themselves in West Berlin, leaving thirteen of us stranded here in the East, thanks to our shiny new Anti-Fascist Protection Barrier. And out of all of them, Marta here is my favorite. East or West."

"I am?"

"As of right now." He swipes the air above her head. "I hereby bestow favorite cousin status upon you. So! Are you just here to see *your* favorite cousin, or has Alma dispatched you on an errand?"

"I brought pork schnitzel."

"Well, then!" Harry pushes himself off the wall. "This meeting is adjourned."

Marta doesn't move. Her heart is pounding. She feels like she's stepped into a dream. "You were talking about crossing the border."

Helmut mutters a curse. He raises his eyes to a pigeon fluttering across the square cutout of gray sky.

Harry smiles. "The furnace is so loud out here, don't you think? I keep telling them, there's something wrong with it. It shouldn't rattle like that, but does anyone care? Does anyone come fix it? Of course not. But it does make it especially hard to hear anything clearly, especially through a metal door."

Marta brings her hands up to her brother's scarf, slides them into its fuzzy folds. "You were talking about Stefan too," she says. "I heard you say he was betrayed."

Harry blinks. He shakes his head. The smile is plastered to his face.

To her surprise, Helmut is the one to speak. "Stefan Dietrich was your brother?" His voice is softer now, the gravel chewed down to a paste.

"Yes."

"I'm sorry," Helmut says. "I mourned him. It was a brave thing he did."

"It was a *stupid* thing," Marta says. A flash of anger, red and raw: Who is this strange man to mourn her brother, to call what he did brave, when what he did took him away from her family forever? *Helmut* is not the one who has to live with Stefan's absence. He does not walk past the silent museum-room with its paperback books and swim trunks draped across the dresser, held in place with snow globe paperweights from Latvia.

Sure, brave. Easy for him to say.

She knows the blame should lie with the trapos who shot her brother. And the nameless, faceless men who gave the order. But she can't help but be angry at Stefan, as angry as she's ever been at anyone. And at the same time, this anger is laced with shame. How can she be mad at her brother when he's the one who got killed? She wishes there were some way to make sense of it all.

Beginning with that ugly barbed wire wall cutting her street in half.

"And if you try to go to West Berlin too," she continues, "it's *extra* stupid because you know what's going to happen. At least there's a chance we can see Markus and our other cousins again someday, when things go back to the way they were. But Stefan's just gone. Forever. And if they catch you, you'll be gone forever too." She meets her cousin's eyes. "Then who's going to build the new freight cars for the Piko on Christmas?"

Marta watches her cousin's smile fade. He seems to lose a whole decade of boyishness in one moment, slipping back into his grown-up skin. He scratches his nose, then the corner of his eye. He pulls his finger away and examines a tiny glob of mush, then wipes his finger on the wall. "Is Gerhard still here?" he asks Marta quietly.

The question surprises her. It's as if these two grown men are out here hiding from a ten-year-old boy.

"He just left for school," Marta says. She looks from Harry to Helmut. She feels like she's missing an important piece of information. "Why?"

A pained look crosses his face. "Gerhard has joined the Young Pioneers."

Helmut looks uncomfortable, but he doesn't say a word. A siren cuts through the hum of the furnace and fades down Bernauer Strasse.

Marta looks from her cousin to Helmut. Then she bursts out laughing. "The scouts?" She pictures the Young Pioneer boys at her school, dressed in their blue trousers, white shirts, and red neckties. "Half my class is in the Young Pioneers. They recycle paper and march in parades and swim in the Orankesee."

The dream she walked into now seems more like an elaborate joke. Harry is fond of pranks—maybe she's on the receiving end of one now.

Most of the parents she knows are proud of their kids for being Young Pioneers.

Harry shakes his head. "Maybe before the wall went up, yes. Sidewalk cleanups and nature hikes. But now they've become little spies. Just last week, Gerhard and his Young Pioneer friends climbed up on the roof"—he points above his head—"and turned all the TV antennas so they no longer pick up the Western broadcasts." He slaps a palm against the wall behind him. "They're molding my son into quite the little fanatic. You know what he says to me every night before he goes to bed? *For peace and socialism be ready.*"

"Always ready," Marta says, completing the Young Pioneers' slogan.

Helmut clears his throat, churning gravel. He glares at Marta. "You one of them too?"

"No," she says. "But everybody knows their little sayings." She looks from her cousin to Helmut. The two men both look deadly serious. She glances up at the little square patch of sky, half expecting to see a bucket of water perched on a ledge with a rope hanging down. Gotcha!

But there's nothing. Not a dream and not a practical joke. Reality.

Okay.

"Can't you just make him quit the Pioneers?" Marta says. She doesn't understand the problem. After all, Gerhard is *ten*, and Harry is his father.

"That's the thing, Marta—since they cut our city in half, everything's upside down! I don't know who he's talking to, or who's been talking to *him*.

The central committee of the Pioneers, the heads of these youth groups—they answer to the Stasi. You think those kids got the idea to turn the antennas back East on their own? A few weeks ago, the only thing Gerhard cared about was model trains. Now there might as well be a secret policeman living in my house!"

"Enough, Harry," Helmut says, his eye straying to Marta.

Marta feels the man's scrutiny like a wave of pressure on her skull. She fights the urge to leave the air shaft and head back home. She looks to her cousin, who's gone tight-lipped. When she meets his eyes, he looks away.

"I'm sorry," he says stiffly. "I spoke out of turn. Forgive me, Marta. I'm pleased that Gerhard is part of such an important movement for our young people to love and value the state that makes such a free and wonderful life possible. Now, about that schnitzel . . ."

"Why are you being weird? Do you think I'm a Stasi spy too?"

Helmut holds up a palm. "Nobody's saying that. Nobody's saying anything at all. We're just out here getting some air."

"I *hate* the Stasi." Harry's eyes go wide. Helmut stares impassively. Words tumble out faster than she can think—traitorous words, words that nobody ever says aloud, words that could easily land her in an interrogation cell. She can scarcely believe what she's saying.

"I hate the wall."

Okay.

"I hate the trapos."

Okay.

"I hate the SED and the stupid Konsum that only has bananas like twice a year. And I hate the stupid field trips to factories every Saturday and I hate that our cousin Markus is *right over there*"—she points—"but we can't ever visit him or talk to him.

"Most of all I hate my stupid brother for getting himself killed." She turns to her cousin. "And now *you're* going to leave us too." Her vision blurs with tears. "And I don't want you to leave, and I don't want you to die, and I don't want to hate you too, Harry. I love you, and Monika and Ingrid and Hans and Joachim and even stupid Gerhard!"

She can't believe what she's saying. The shame grows into something inescapable. Her face grows hot. The scarf feels like it's choking her.

Harry looks pained. He glances at Helmut. The big man shakes his head: *no.*

"We have to trust someone," Harry tells him.

"I don't even trust *you*, Harry," Helmut says. "Nothing personal." But he doesn't say anything else. And when Harry begins to talk, Helmut doesn't stop him.

"I'm not going to leave you," Harry explains to Marta, "or your mother, or your father, or Monika, or the children, or any of the others." He sighs. "I'm going to take you with me. *All* of you. And I need your help."

Night falls on Bernauer Strasse. Streetlights come to life. Barbed wire glimmers. Pedestrians shuffle home, hands stuffed down deep in pockets, long scarves trailing.

Kneeling on a cushion, Marta rests her elbows on the back of the sofa and watches the street. Cold air sneaks through the gaps in the ancient windowpane. Penelope comes and goes, nudging Marta with the stuffed squeaky toys she carries in her mouth. Look! Look! A sausage, a cat, a green pepper! But Marta's in no mood to play. Penelope retreats to gnaw on a rawhide stick.

Helmut's words linger in her mind.

I don't even trust you, Harry.

Down below, Herr Schmidt steps outside and pulls the collar of his coat up to cover his neck. He stops to talk to a neighbor, bends at the waist to greet her little boy, then ambles away toward the Mauerpark. Puffs of steam trail his head like ribbons. A fine mist hangs in the air, and as the evening deepens, it thickens into a gentle snowfall.

Trust. Marta has never really pondered it before. Not like this, anyway. It has always felt like something that either *is*—she trusts her family—or *isn't*—she doesn't trust Herr Schmidt.

But after today, trust seems much fuzzier and harder to define. Helmut says he doesn't trust Harry, yet they're planning an escape together. And Helmut certainly doesn't trust *her*. Yet he's going along with this plan, in which she is now a crucial part.

Meanwhile, Harry no longer trusts his own son Gerhard. So, trust isn't really an all-or-nothing, automatic belief in someone. It's more of a free-floating thing that knits people together in strange ways—even when it's broken. She imagines a thin web falling over the city from the Brandenburg Gate to Potsdam.

"Have you seen my work shoes?" her mother calls from the bedroom. She's heading to her overnight shift in a few minutes. The worst assignment in the factory. The hours nobody wants that the labor exchange saves for people who used to work in the West.

"Sock drawer!" her father replies. Marta's heart sinks. His voice comes from Stefan's room. The museum. She has seen him in there before, lying on the bed, gazing up at the ceiling, clutching one of Stefan's swimming trophies.

"What are my shoes doing in the sock drawer?" her mother asks.

"I don't remember."

A drawer opens and closes and a moment later her mother emerges in her uniform—a garment beamed in from another decade that is half blouse, half apron, with a collar that looks cross-stitched with black loops of yarn. Marta watches her in the window's reflection.

"Well," she says, "I'm off." Penelope raises her head, stretches, yawns, then goes back to her rawhide.

"Mutti." Marta turns to face her. "How do you know when to stop trusting someone?"

Her mother slides her arms into her overcoat. "That's a complicated question to ask me on my way out. Where is this coming from?"

"Harry says Stefan was betrayed."

Her mother pauses at the door. "Why were you talking to Harry about Stefan?"

"I don't know. It just came up."

Her mother gives her the Teacher Look, which is a kind of furrowed-brow scrutiny that makes Marta feel like she's about to be called up to the board to solve a math problem in front of the whole class. "If someone brings up your brother, it's best to say you don't want to talk about it."

"It was just Harry."

"It doesn't matter who it is."

Marta thinks for a moment. "Do you not trust him?"

Her mother shoulders her purse. "I'm going to be late. Make sure you take Penelope down to the sidewalk before you go to bed. I don't want to come home to any surprises on the carpet."

"Poop surprises."

Her mother sighs. "Yes, Marta. Poop surprises." She blows a kiss from the doorway. Marta catches it in the air and slaps it on her forehead. Then her mother is gone.

Now she just has to wait for her father to retreat to his bedroom. Then she can do what Harry asked of her.

She turns back to the window. The snow is thicker now, falling at an angle and sticking to the street. A boy and a girl come running from the building next door, racing straight toward the barbed wire barrier. Marta holds her breath. She tightens her grip on the back of the sofa. The girl pulls ahead. The boy calls out to her. When she turns to look over her shoulder, he sprints into the lead. They turn sharply, just before skidding into the wire at the base of the fence line, and run along Bernauer Strasse. A *grepo*—border policeman—in his green uniform admonishes them as they run past. Their laughter fades as they vanish into the night, leaving nothing but faint boot prints in their wake. The grepo watches them go, then resumes his patrol, shaking his head.

Marta exhales and loosens her grip on the sofa. Just neighbor kids playing outside, like she and Stefan used to do on snowy nights. She watches the grepo move smartly, picking up his assigned route. She eyes the rifle slung over his shoulder. She doesn't know anything about firearms. Was it the same kind of rifle that killed Stefan?

Okay.

How strange to think that if those two kids hadn't swerved at the last minute—if they'd catapulted themselves into the wire, fought through the deadly tangles, scrambled over the borderline—that same grepo who shook his head in amusement at their little race would have unslung his rifle, barked a command, and ended their lives.

Two more lines on the chalkboard.

"I thought you might want to look through these." Marta tears herself away from the window at the sound of her father's voice. He comes into the living room wearing a tweed suit. He sets a stack of brightly colored comic books down on the coffee table.

Her brother's collection of *Mosaik*. The never-ending adventures of the Digedags, who pop up everywhere from ancient Rome to pirate ships to modern-day America. Marta is pretty sure they're supposed to be lovable mischief-makers, but she's always found them a little creepy. Stefan was a huge fan—though he could never properly explain to her what, exactly, they were. Roly-poly adults? Weird-looking children? Fantastical sprites?

"Oh," Marta says, "thanks. Are you going to a funeral?" The last time she saw her father in a suit was at the memorial for her brother. There had been no casket. The authorities had insisted he be cremated.

His hand smooths out his lurid green tie. "I'm going to get some stamps."

Marta cocks her head. "Stamps?"

"I'm starting a collection."

Marta has no idea what to say. Her father has only ever had one hobby: swimming.

"Okay," she says, after a moment. It doesn't make any sense. Buying stamps at this hour? In a suit?

Her father reads the look on her face. "I'm meeting a gentleman about some rare finds."

"Ooookay," she says again.

"You'll keep an eye on Penelope? Make sure she doesn't burn the place down? I won't be long."

Marta picks up the top issue of *Mosaik*. The Digedags are visiting the Kremlin, the seat of Soviet power in Moscow. The largest of the three, Dig or Dag (she's not sure), is climbing one of the building's famous onion domes.

"I'm just gonna look through some of these."

Her father looks down at the pile of comics. For a moment, he seems to lose himself. "You know, when he was younger, your brother's favorite was the one where the Digedags go to the rain forest. They ride a giant toucan. I used to read it to him before bed." His face hints at a smile. "Every night." He bends down and shuffles through the comics, fanning them out on the coffee table like a deck of cards. "I was so sick of it." He slides one after another aside. Then he reaches the end of the collection and fans them out the other way.

"Papa," Marta says.

He searches again through the glossy booklets. "It has to be here somewhere."

"It's okay."

He shakes his head, glares darkly at the comics, and stacks them into a neat pile. Then he looks helplessly at Marta. "Every night. The same story."

He straightens up and takes his coat from the hook. "Well, anyway," he says, and goes out with the coat clutched in his fist, sleeves dragging along the floor.

Marta turns back to the window. Half a minute later her father emerges onto the sidewalk. The grepo retraces his steps in the opposite direction. The snow has fallen to cover the tracks of the two kids. When her father is out of sight, Marta goes into the kitchen. It smells like boiled cabbage. The telephone is in its cradle on the counter.

She picks it up and dials the number Harry had her memorize. She wasn't allowed to write anything down. The prefix means she's calling someone in the Neukölln district.

Her heart begins to pound. She leans against the counter and holds the receiver to her ear, mentally rehearsing the code words she's supposed to use. It doesn't matter what she says around them, as long as she inserts them into the conversation in the proper order.

A woman picks up on the other end. "Hallo, Schneider."

Marta's mind goes blank.

"Hallo?" the woman repeats. "Who is this?"

Marta takes a deep breath. *For Stefan*, she thinks. "*Guten abend*, Frau Schneider," she says. "This is the ghost of Christmas past . . ."

Stasi Headquarters
The House of a Thousand Eyes

"This is the ghost of Christmas past."

The voice belongs to Marta Dietrich, twelve years old. Agent Lothar Muller has extensive notes on her family spread out before him on his desk, but he does not consult them. As busy as he is, doubling his workload since the wall went up, the case is fresh in his mind.

He just saw Marta this morning, after all.

Across the landscape of photographs and documents, his assistant, Klaus, watches the reel-to-reel recorder spin as it imprints the girl's voice on its thin strand of tape.

There's a long pause. He can hear the other party—this "Schneider," though of course that won't be her real name—breathing softly.

Klaus can't help but stare at the machine as it does its work. It makes him seem like a child.

Muller's own eyes drift around his windowless office, taking in the linoleum floor he polishes himself because the cleaning service does an inadequate job, the mustard-colored walls, the framed portrait of Walter Ulbricht, first secretary of the Socialist Unity Party and leader of East Germany.

Well, not "leader," exactly, Muller reminds himself. We don't use that fascist term—*führer*—in the GDR.

Nevertheless, that's just what Ulbricht is.

"I'm surprised to hear from you," this Frau Schneider says. He makes a note to have Klaus run the alias. "Christmas isn't for another few weeks."

Another pause. He thinks he can hear the girl whispering. At first he can't figure it out—is she talking to someone else in the room with her? But then he realizes she's practicing what she's going to say.

"It's coming early this year in Dresden," Marta says. Her voice quivers.

"All right," Frau Schneider says, low and soothing. She's done this before and is trying to get the girl to relax. A wave of satisfaction washes over Muller. If they're dealing with a pro, it's likely someone they already have under surveillance. It shouldn't be too hard to tighten the noose. It's just a matter of how long he wants to let it dangle before it chokes them. "Do you know what color stocking you'd like?"

"Green."

"Wonderful. And how is everything else going for you?"

"Good," Marta says. "Very good. Fine." Muller smirks. The girl's exhausted all her code words, and now the more seasoned agent is trying to make this pathetic conversation end naturally.

"All right," Frau Schneider says. "Have a nice evening."

"Oh. You too."

Click.

Muller waits five seconds, giving the tape some dead air at the end just to be safe. Then he presses the button to end the recording. Klaus is busy scribbling notes, a lock of his wavy blond hair dangling in front of his spectacles like a windshield wiper on one of the army's Kraz 255 trucks. While his assistant takes his detailed impressions of the phone call for his report, Muller swivels in his chair to the table next to his desk. His hand moves across all manner of hats, wigs, and glasses—including the disguise he wore earlier today. A shaggy-haired American beatnik look. One of his favorites. He removes the lid from a jar and selects a candy cane. He begins to peel the plastic wrapper. Klaus looks up from his notebook and places his pen down like a student completing a test.

"So," Muller says, dropping the wrapper into the bin under his desk, "give me your assessment."

It is part of his job to oversee Klaus's advancement in the Ministry of State

Security. Whether the young man is more suited to an analyst's or field agent's position remains to be seen.

"The girl is clumsy, which is to be expected—she is a child playing an adult's game."

"Don't underestimate our socialist youth."

"Of course not, sir."

"Stick to the facts. Psychology, emotion, opinion—we can't deny ourselves these things; we're human, after all. But simply let them float like wine corks on an ocean of the facts."

Klaus checks his notes. Muller pops the straight end of the candy cane into his mouth. The sweet sugary peppermint is calming. He savors it, turning it slowly like a chicken on a spit. Gradually, he applies more force with his teeth.

"Ghost," Klaus says. "Christmas. Dresden. Green. I believe these are the signal words. They were fairly easy to pick out, due to the girl's obvious inexperience. There was little attempt made to pad the conversation with natural speech patterns."

Muller withdraws the candy cane. "Remember the Mitte operation? The Oktoberfest group? Their endless prattle was nauseating."

"How could I forget, sir?" Klaus glances at the clock on the wall. His leg bounces. Muller notes his impatience. "Shall I cross-reference these words with our database?"

"In a moment. Would you like a candy cane, Klaus?"

"No thank you, sir."

"Do you have somewhere you need to be? Is it your girlfriend's birthday?"

"I don't have a girlfriend."

"I know that." He places the wet, shiny end of the candy cane in a clean ashtray and leans back in his chair. "You seem a little on edge. Do you find this assignment beneath you? Speak freely."

Klaus purses his thin, bloodless lips. Muller watches his subordinate intently. The invitation to "speak freely" is such an intriguing dilemma for an up-and-coming Stasi agent. Especially one sitting inside the House of a Thousand Eyes. Surveillance is like a prism: reflections upon reflections, casting changing colors on the wall. Whatever Klaus says could be recorded, added to his file, used against him in the future. Klaus knows this. But he also knows that shutting down entirely—refusing to place any trust at all in his mentor inside the Ministry—will grind his career to a halt.

Klaus knows that Muller knows this.

Muller knows that Klaus knows that Muller knows this.

Prisms within prisms.

"It's like I said. My gut reaction is that Marta is just a girl playing a game she doesn't understand."

"She is a link in a larger chain."

"I know, but—"

"What about this case in particular is making you so uncomfortable?"

Klaus eyes the candy cane, shiny and sticky in the glass ashtray. He takes in the files spread out on the desk—photographs of Marta's brother, Stefan, now deceased, thanks to the patriotic informing of two of his teammates on his school's freestyle relay. Photographs of Marta's cousin, this man Harry Dietrich, the DR locomotive engineer, whose apartment she visited earlier today.

"Her brother has only been dead for a month," Klaus says at last. Muller raises an eyebrow, impressed with his subordinate's candor. Though this display of sensitivity, as if they're old friends at the beer hall, isn't a good sign for Klaus's ability to stomach the work of the secret police.

"I see," Muller says. "And because of this recent death, you feel sympathy for her."

"I'm not suggesting that our border guards were wrong to shoot him!"

Klaus says quickly. "Of course, such strict border control measures are necessary. But from her perspective, it's still a family tragedy. At the age of twelve, I can see why she might be struggling to process the event. That is, she might not be thinking clearly about her actions and their consequences."

Muller retrieves the candy cane and works on it with his front teeth, spiraling the tip into a sharp point. Then he replaces it in the ashtray. Walter Ulbricht stares down from his portrait. Footsteps come and go in the corridor outside his office. Colleagues headed for the Ministry's special supermarket, picking up some groceries before the commute home—ripe fruits and vegetables you won't find in the average East Berlin grocery store.

"Your own brother died when you were fourteen," Muller says. It isn't a question. He knows the details of his subordinate's life inside and out. Klaus isn't surprised, of course.

"Yes."

"Making you an only child overnight."

"Yes."

"So, because you remember what it was like to lose Karsten, you're identifying closely with the pain Marta Dietrich is feeling."

"It's not clouding my judgment, if that's what you're asking, sir."

"I haven't asked you a thing."

At this, both men fall silent. Muller gathers his thoughts. Buttons must be pushed, levers pulled. After all, in the end, Klaus's performance will reflect upon him. It is his job to mold this young man into a weapon the Stasi can point at whomever it wishes.

"For thirteen years," Muller says, "we allowed Western corruption to move freely back and forth across our weak and porous border. And all the while, Herr Ulbricht"—he nods at the portrait—"advocated for a stronger position. A real barrier, to keep out the insidious creep of capitalism and greed. He never wavered in his belief that the only way to achieve true socialism is to first cut out the cancer of the West. And when you cut out a cancer, you must be vigilant, lest it return! The minute your attention wavers, the corruption begins to fester once again. We are already seeing this happen, are we not, with Western agents finding new ways to reach across into the lives of our citizens, to find new ways to undermine our great mission? You and I have exposed several of these plots already." He pauses, letting Klaus take the reins for a moment.

"The tunnels," Klaus says, fondly remembering their biggest success. "The fake passports." Then his face turns sour. "And the sewers."

Muller allows himself a smile. "Not quite as glorious, that last one. But necessary work." Muller feels the satisfaction creep in. He can read Klaus's face—the young man loves the glory of exposing these escape operations. Arresting filthy traitors, dragging them out of their makeshift tunnels. He presses harder. "And now we've been given a new kind of plot. One that we haven't seen before—and it's ours!"

"Trains," Klaus says.

Muller nods. "Thanks to our work on the sewer operation, and the tunnels, and the passports, we've already been noticed by Supervisor Mielke. Ninety-three thousand employees of the Ministry, and I have it on good authority that he has personally used our names in very high-level meetings as examples of agents on the rise. But every attempt at border crossing we've seen so far—swimming the harbor, crashing through with a truck like that latest business—will be nothing compared to this one. Think of it, Klaus! An entire train! When we put a stop to it, they'll be falling over themselves to promote us. They'll probably give us our own houses in Potsdam!"

He can see the dreamy look cross Klaus's face. He bites off half the candy cane and chews it to bits.

"If we do this right—if we can use Marta Dietrich like an injection of poison into the plan—perhaps we can prevent the whole thing without spilling a drop of blood. Would you prefer that?"

Klaus brightens. "Of course!"

Muller holds up a finger. "But if we cannot—if circumstances force us to take lethal action—then we must be equally comfortable with that outcome."

Klaus composes himself. "Of course."

"Remember what our esteemed British counterparts say: *In intelligence work, the ends justify the means.*"

Klaus frowns. "How do you know what British agents say?"

Muller smiles. "Klaus. Come on. How do you think? Now, you are dismissed. Go find yourself a girlfriend."

Klaus hesitates. Muller sighs. "What is it?"

"I had a dream last night."

"When I said *speak freely*, there was a limit."

But Klaus plows ahead. "I dreamt of the future. The wall had grown into something monstrous. It spanned from the Baltic Sea to the Adriatic, a solid block of concrete ten stories high, slicing down through Germany and Czechoslovakia and Hungary and Yugoslavia."

Muller shrugs. "Perhaps you caught a glimpse of how things will be one day."

"Do you think our people would accept such a thing?"

Muller laughs. "My boy, whether they accept it or not has nothing to do with it. People will get used to anything over time."

This is the wall!"

Frau Petrovsky's wooden pointer comes down with a sharp *thwack* on the chessboard. "Here!" She moves the pointer along the ragged line of pawns. It doesn't look much like a wall. "To here!" Her Russian-accented German rings out in the cold, cramped room on the sixth floor of the academy. "In chess, walls need not be straight lines. They need not look like walls at all. They can zig and zag across the board. They can be made up of empty space. In chess, the wall is an *idea*."

Kurt Muller catches his friend Lina's eye across their chessboard. Her face is entirely blank. Then she purses her lips and shows her top front teeth in a quick impression of a chipmunk. Kurt tries to hold it together, but a laugh slips out. He attempts to cover it with a cough.

Frau Petrovsky puts her hands on her hips. The pointer sticks out of her closed fist like a bayonet, pointed directly at his head.

"Herr Muller, demonstrate to me the Nimzo-Indian Defense, please."

"Um," Kurt says.

"Lina has opened with"—she glares distastefully at the chessboard—"some kind of weak bourgeois claptrap. Don't you think an aggressive Soviet-style response is appropriate in this situation?"

"Yes, Frau Petrovsky," Kurt says. But he doesn't move. His vision swims. His head goes light. When he's playing against Lina in his living room, with no one looking over his shoulder, he's the equal of any twelve-year-old chess player in East Berlin—and a good many of the older players too. It's only here, on Tuesday afternoons at the academy, under the all-seeing eye of this terrifying Soviet lady, that Kurt suddenly forgets everything.

Nimzo-Indian Defense? Aggressive Soviet chess styles?

He can barely remember how his knights and rooks are supposed to move across the board. He might as well be playing checkers. He imagines picking up a bishop and making it leapfrog over a pawn—king me! Despite his nerves, he stifles another laugh.

Frau Petrovsky mutters something in Russian. Kurt imagines it has to do with self-discipline, and respect, and how in Moscow they would never put up with this. How today's youth are just as lazy as the Westerners, and so on. Then she walks away, swinging the pointer, moving down the row of chessboards and time clocks set up on the long cafeteria-style table.

Kurt exhales. On the wall over Lina's shoulder, the portrait of East German chess champion Wolfgang Uhlmann looks down at him. Uhlmann's smirk seems to say, *Come on, kid. You can do better than that.* At least Uhlmann looks like he might appreciate Lina's chipmunk face. Next to Uhlmann, a portrait of Vladimir Lenin, founder and first leader of the Soviet Union, glowers down at him with cold eyes and a pointy beard that makes him look like a devilish puppet.

Kurt doesn't think Vladimir Lenin would find the chipmunk face very funny.

Lina advances a knight and hits the clock. She makes her face completely blank—too blank. She's up to something. Kurt studies the pieces. He recognizes her so-called bourgeois opening, but he can't quite figure it out. Lina's style of play is sly and mischievous, like her: traps within traps, wrapped up in jokes.

Now that Frau Petrovsky is on the other side of the room, tormenting another pair of students, Kurt allows himself to look up from the board and out the window.

The academy is situated on a hill in the East Berlin district of Treptow. The apartment blocks closest to the wall were cleared out long before Kurt was born, and the academy building is one of the few places in the neighborhood that still looks out into West Berlin. In fact, from this very seat, Kurt can see for an entire kilometer into the Western neighborhood of Neukölln, with its leafy streets and well-kept buildings. From there, the thin blue line of the Landwehr Canal snakes farther westward into Kreuzberg. Kurt squints into the hazy smog that hangs over Berlin like a tired storm cloud drooping down to earth.

Somewhere in Kreuzberg, his parents are going about their day. He wonders if they're thinking of him right now.

"Kurt!" Lina hisses. "Eyes on the game. I don't want to hear excuses when I beat you."

Pigeons, startled by a car horn, flutter up from the wall and flap in formation into West Berlin.

"It's your move!" Lina's voice recedes to a low background hum. He watches the pigeons get smaller until they're nothing but black dots in the sky, vanishing into the West.

How easy it would be to cross the border if he had wings!

He'd love to see the look on Frau Petrovsky's face if he made a run for the window, dove out into the air, caught a westerly jet stream, and soared, laughing, over the wall. Border guards too stunned to raise their rifles. Crowds gathering below, pointing up in disbelief. Alighting upon that grand old apartment building in Kreuzberg he's only ever seen in smuggled photographs, gliding right into his parents' window.

I'm here now. Forever.

Kurt is vaguely aware of Lina reaching across the board, moving a rook for him, tapping his side of the game clock. His eyes sweep back through Kreuzberg and across the deadly expanse of the wall.

Really, *wall* is too simple a word for what the barrier has become, over time. Kurt has seen photos of the early days of the wall in one of his grandfather Lothar Muller's albums. In 1961, it was little more than a barbed wire fence. He's heard his grandfather's stories about how the East Germans put up the whole thing in one night. Now it's hard to imagine a time when it wasn't the massively fortified, heavily guarded river of concrete and steel that runs through the city.

Even from this height, it's hard to take in all the sections of the wall at once. He moves his eyes through it piece by piece, like a chess match.

The opening: The drab concrete hinterland wall, rising above the patchwork of garden plots at the very edge of Treptow. Little squares for households to grow their own meager supply of vegetables. Over the first wall and you run into the border signal fence—coiled barbed wire and mesh, wired and alarmed.

The middle game: Welcome to the tank traps on the other side of the wire. *Höckersperren* (dragon's teeth) and *flächensperren* (steel bars with spikes). Squeeze through them and you find yourself exposed along the supply road lit by floodlights and watched by observation towers that sprout like grim fungus every 300 meters.

The end game: Please enjoy the death strip, the flat sandy stretch that leads straight into a ditch to trap any vehicles that somehow make it that far. And for anyone else still alive and miraculously not riddled with bullets, there's the final concrete wall topped with its thick rounded pipe to make it nearly impossible to climb over.

Again, he imagines spreading his wings and soaring over the top of it all. He is vaguely aware that Lina has given up trying to get his attention and is now moving his pieces, punching his game clock, taking turn after turn for him. In his mind he rises above the smog and into crisp, clean air with the warm sun on his face.

Lina's palm slaps the game clock with a triumphant flourish. Kurt's daydream dissolves. He finds himself back in the cold room on the sixth floor, staring across the table at his friend. She grins at him, sits back in her chair, and slides a stray wisp of her blond hair behind her ear.

"Checkmate!"

The four-door Opel glides up to the curb outside the Treptow Chess Academy. The driver's window rolls down and Kurt's older brother, Franz, beckons.

"Come on, come on!" he calls out, even though Kurt and Lina are already hurrying over to the sleek black car. "I'm going to be late for work."

"You say that every time you drive us home," Lina points out, *home* being the same apartment building, one floor apart. She slides into the back seat, and Kurt piles in after her. The inside of the car smells like the starch his brother uses to keep his grepo uniform crisp. Franz hits the gas before Kurt can even shut the door, and the nimble little car joins the late afternoon traffic that creeps along the south end of Treptower Park.

"Yeah," Kurt says, turning to watch the wall recede, then vanish, as Franz turns a corner. "Chill out."

"*Chill out.*" He mocks Kurt's voice. "Do you know what our

grandfather would say if he heard you spouting American slang?"

"I don't care," Kurt mutters.

Franz darts in front of an old Trabant the color of the overripe pears they get at the Konsum. The Trabant's driver leans on its horn. Its weak bleating makes Kurt think of a cartoon tongue splatting out onto the ground. Franz changes lanes. His hands are tight around the wheel and his shoulders are hunched as he leans forward in his seat. While the Trabant sputters and coughs, the Opel hums softly—a shark in a sea of goldfish. Its very presence on the road is a quiet boast. It whispers: *Stasi.*

"Not that it's any of your business, Chuckles"—Franz's nickname for Kurt, which he always makes a point to use in front of Lina—"but I'm running late today because they've called the guards in early tonight for an all-hands meeting." He upshifts and guns the engine, merging onto the Adlergestell, the longest road in all of Berlin. They are headed southeast toward the district of Adlershof, and home.

If East Berlin is a chessboard, thinks Kurt, then Adlershof is where the bishops are stationed. Not quite the kings and queens, but the ones who influence the powerful pieces—and move diagonally to evade capture. Adlershof is home to the guard regiment of the Ministry of State Security—the Stasi's elite commando units. His older brother's dream job. He's already started training while he works as a grepo.

"All hands," Lina says. She splays her fingers and waggles them, giving Kurt's shoulder a series of smacks. "All hands, all hands, all hands."

"Quit it, Lina!" He laughs and waggles his hands in defense.

"That's enough!" Franz barks from the driver's seat in his most authoritative grepo voice. For a moment, Lina and Kurt freeze, still as mannequins in the back seat. Then Lina's smirk creeps across her face. Kurt loses it. They burst out laughing.

"*All hands* simply means *everyone on the night shift* must report for a meeting," Franz explains through gritted teeth. "It indicates that something very important is coming up. An event that requires a change in protocol."

"Are they building another wall?" Kurt asks. Outside the window, East Berlin blurs past as the car moves through an unbroken sheet of gray. They pass massive *plattenbau* apartment buildings, concrete housing blocks that look like they've sprung from the mind of the most boring architect in the world. He thinks of his view of West Berlin. It's like a black-and-white television that suddenly and miraculously picks up a color station.

At least his mother and father are living in color.

"Joke around all you want, Chuckles," Franz says. He pulls another quick lane switch and accelerates down the Adlergestell, leaving a line of Trabants in the dust. "But if you understood anything about duty, and honor, and sacrifice for one's country, you wouldn't find the wall so funny."

"I *don't* find it funny," Kurt says. "Mom and Dad are on the other side of it."

"Who?" Franz says sharply.

"Mom," Kurt says slowly. "And Dad."

"Who?" Franz says again, pounding his fist on the car horn and flashing his lights to urge the driver in front of him out of the way.

Kurt sighs. "Nobody."

"Right," Franz says. "Nobody at all."

Kurt lets his attention drift from the world outside to the leather headrest of the driver's seat in front of him. He resists the urge to hammer his fist against it while he screams out their parents' forbidden names. But what would be the point? They've had this conversation so many times. His brother's ears are closed.

Lina lifts her wrist so that her hand dangles to the car seat, extends two fingers in an upside-down peace sign, and makes them walk like little legs across the back seat. Then she bops Kurt's knee.

"You know what *is* funny, Franz?" Lina says. She gives Kurt a look—*wait for it*. She's trying to change the subject to save Kurt from dwelling on his parents. This happens every time. And every time, he's glad for it. "Your hat."

Franz ignores her. "There's nothing funny about safeguarding true socialism," he says. "I can only hope that this will become clear to you as you get older. But it probably won't unless somebody beats it into you." His eyes search for Kurt's in the rearview. "You know," he says, sly satisfaction creeping into his voice, "we shot a traitor the other day."

Kurt glances over at Lina, who rolls her eyes. When Franz says *we,* it could mean anything from the grepos to the trapos to the Stasi to the army to some random policeman on the street. It's as if his nineteen-year-old brother, who's been a border guard for exactly one year, has been absorbed cleanly into the huge, gelatinous mass that is East German authority.

Kurt doesn't say anything.

"Want to know what happened?" Franz says at last.

"No."

Franz hits an open stretch of road, shifts into high gear, and hits the gas. The Opel eats up the pavement. The plattenbau rush past. Kurt imagines them all connected, kilometer after kilometer of dull housing blocks—and inside them, a labyrinth of corridors, tunnels, upside-down staircases, doorways to nowhere . . .

"He was a real criminal mastermind, this one," Franz says. The enthusiasm in his voice makes it seem like he's talking about a heart-pounding, last-second goal in a football game. "Tried to waltz right through the checkpoint with a forged passport. When we asked him to step out of the queue, he took off running—not back into the East where he came from, but *through* the checkpoint itself." Franz shakes his head. A smile plays across his lips. It's a fond memory. "What a madman. Anyway, we put eleven holes in him before he got very far. The three guards that fired their rifles got champagne and a weekend trip to Mecklenburg," Franz adds wistfully.

His other dream in life is to shoot a border crosser.

Lina makes a face like, *gross*. Outside, the housing blocks are replaced by sparse greenery. Franz steers the Opel off the busy road and downshifts onto the quieter streets of Adlershof. The Opel bounces across the cobblestones.

"Anyway, everybody already knows what the all-hands meeting is about," Franz boasts.

Kurt imagines his door lock button is actually the switch for an ejector seat. He pictures the roof of the car opening, his rocket-powered seat launching him high above Adlershof and the cloud of smog, flinging him up and away into a world mercifully free of his brother's voice.

"The Swedish prime minister is coming to East Berlin for a state visit with Honecker," Franz says. "We're going to be told to be on our best behavior. I don't know why we should have to put on a show for some capitalist warmonger, but these decisions aren't up to me." He reaches up, adjusts the rearview, then glares at Kurt and Lina in turn. "That's one thing you two kids don't understand about duty—when orders come down from your superior officer, you'd better obey them. Whether you agree with them or not doesn't matter."

The Opel slows. Just ahead, a truck struggles to back into a tight spot. Stalled cars line up behind it.

"The rumor is they'll be suspending the schiessbefehl order while the prime minister is in town," Franz says. Bitterness creeps into his voice.

Kurt, who had been barely listening, perks up. This piece of information pulls him out of the sky, crashes his ejector seat back down into the car. Schiessbefehl suspended? So the guards won't be shooting people who try to cross the border?

"Too many so-called journalists poking their noses in," Franz continues. "I say let them see what the Westerners have forced us to do." He shakes his head. "It's not that I think Honecker is going soft, of course. He's doing what he has to do on the international stage, where people are more squeamish.

Anyway, it's my job to abide by the rules, whatever they are. That's how our country stays strong." Bitterness is replaced by irritation. He gestures at the truck up ahead. "Why can't this guy just park already? I'm running late."

"We heard," Lina says. Kurt stares at her, lost in thought. She makes a face like *What?* Kurt looks away. His brother's talk of suspending schiessbefehl for the prime minister's visit has lodged in his head. At first he can't wrap his mind around it. It's like an itch he can't scratch. But now that they're in Adlershof, land of the bishops, the great chessboard of East Berlin takes shape in his head. Around the margins floats Frau Petrovsky's disembodied voice, urging him to recognize his opening.

This "madman" Franz speaks of—aggressive, spontaneous, on the attack, running headlong through a checkpoint. That is obviously going to end in disaster. But with the shoot-to-kill order suspended, combined with a more cautious, defensive strategy, there just might be a way to cross the border without getting killed.

He closes his eyes and glides across the rooftops of Kreuzberg, a floating eye free to roam the West and find his exiled parents. At the same time, Frau Petrovsky's voice gets louder, reminding him of something so obvious it makes him laugh out loud. He opens his eyes.

"The Berlin Defense!" he exclaims. A strategy that often results in a draw but can usher in the endgame very quickly.

"What about it?" Lina says.

"I'll tell you later."

She makes her face into Frau Petrovsky's stern mask. "Exchange queens early!" she says in the chess instructor's thick Russian accent. Meaning: Cut out all the hemming and hawing of the middle game. Get right down to business.

He can't quite make the plan take shape, but the foundation is there. He just has to find out when the Swedish prime minister is visiting. He's dying to talk to Lina about it. They're almost home.

Up ahead, the truck has finally parked. Kurt can't figure out why his brother isn't moving. He watches, puzzled, as Franz rolls down the window.

"Excuse me!" he calls to three teenagers—two girls and a boy—hanging out in front of a corner store. It's one of those places common in East Berlin, where the window's full of odds and ends in faded packages, but the CLOSED sign is always on the door.

The car behind them honks. Franz ignores it. He leans out the window to make sure the three teenagers notice that a uniformed grepo is glaring at them.

"I thought you were late," Kurt says. Franz ignores him too.

"Punks," Lina says in an awestruck voice, as if she's just spotted aliens.

Kurt can't help but stare along with her. He's *heard* of punks and seen photographs on the news during a special report warning of anti-government threats among youth culture. The newscaster showed a clip of some West Berlin punks bouncing around and smashing into one another at a concert in a sweaty basement. But Kurt has never actually laid eyes on them in real life, not here in the East. And now, here are three real-life punks, hanging out just a few blocks from home!

One of the girls takes off the headphones connected to her portable cassette player. Her hair is dyed the color of a neon sign and teased up into a spiky rat's nest. Dark smudges of makeup encircle her eyes. Interlocking silver rings dangle like a chain from her left ear. Her skirt is striped like a zebra. Her black stockings are torn. The leather belt around her waist and the bracelets on her wrists are studded with silver spikes.

"You need directions to the wall, sir?" she calls out, pointing back toward the Adlergestell. "It's that way. Can't miss it."

Kurt laughs. He's never seen anyone talk to his brother this way. The girl flips the tape in her cassette player.

The driver behind them leans on his horn.

"Move along!" Franz yells at the girl. "There are families with young children who live here."

"What do you think we're going to do?" the girl says. "Eat them?"

"You're disgusting," Franz says. Then he hits the gas.

Kurt stares out the back windshield as the Opel pulls away. The girl puts her headphones back on.

"Those criminals are lucky I'm in a hurry. A few nights in Hohenschönhausen would straighten them right out."

"How do you know they were criminals?" Kurt says.

"Please." Franz cranks the wheel and rounds a tight turn. "Did you see them? Some of them pierce themselves with safety pins, you know. If I ever catch you dressing like a punk, I'll straighten you right out."

Kurt would never say this to Franz, but ever since that news broadcast, he's wondered what it would feel like to walk around in a black leather jacket.

"You got that, Chuckles?" Franz says. "Zero tolerance."

"Uh-huh." Were there any chess-playing punks? Maybe he could be the first. "I got it."

"Good." The Opel pulls up in front of their building. Ordinary and nondescript, but mercifully not quite as bland as a plattenbau. "I made spaetzle for dinner. There's a plate waiting for you upstairs."

"Thanks."

Kurt and Lina get out of the car and head for the front door.

"Hey!" Franz calls after him.

Kurt turns around.

"Watch *Der Schwarze Kanal* so you can let me know what I miss."

"Okay."

"And do your homework!"

"I will."

"I love you, Kurt."

"Love you too."

ina scrapes up the last of the spaetzle and shovels the heaping forkful into her mouth.

"This is better than my oma's. Why is your brother such an amazing cook?"

Kurt makes his body into a tense statue and pinches his face. "Discipline! Self-control! Hard work!"

She laughs and wipes her mouth with the back of her hand. Kurt clears their plates from the table, crosses the linoleum floor, and drops them into the sink. His eye catches a little blotch of red on the backsplash tiles—a tiny splatter of tomato sauce, dried and hardened from the last meal his mother cooked in this kitchen, seven months ago now.

The last lingering bit of their parents that Franz hasn't scrubbed away.

The radio, tuned to SFB (broadcast out of West Berlin, how his brother would rage at that!) plays a song by the Irish band U2. It's called "Where the

Streets Have No Name," and it makes Kurt think of a never-ending city much like Berlin, stretching away into infinity, where its weary citizens quit bothering to name their streets after a while. Or maybe they just ran out of things to name them after.

He turns to watch Lina zone out to the shimmering guitar noise that introduces the song. She bobs her head when the drums come in. He follows her eyes to the wall calendar Franz put up in place of their father's bird photographs. The January page has a portrait of East German head of state Erich Honecker looking very serious.

"Did you see his jeans?" Lina asks abruptly as U2's vocalist, Bono, begins singing.

"Who, Erich Honecker?"

"The boy today. One of the punks your brother yelled at."

"What about them?"

"They were Levi's. I'm sure of it."

"Black market, then."

Lina sighs. "I want a pair so bad."

"I'm thinking a leather jacket for me."

Lina frowns and studies him. Kurt has that tingly under-a-microscope feeling. He imagines becoming a caterpillar, inching across the floor, encountering crumbs the size of bread loaves, taking refuge under the stove, emerging a few days later as a butterfly, making his way West, over the wall, flap flap flap, unseen and unremarked upon by grepos like his brother.

"Hello!" Lina waves her hand at him. "I said, *I think it would look good on you*. You're off in Kurt-land even more than usual today. I've never finished an entire chess game for you before. You're lucky Frau Petrovsky was distracted."

Kurt looks at his reflection in the television screen. That punk they saw earlier looked pretty intimidating in his leather jacket, which clung to his broad-shouldered frame. On Kurt, a jacket like that would dangle like a coat on a scarecrow. He puts his hands on his hips. His reflection is all sharp, knobbly angles. "You really think a leather jacket would look good on me?"

"Depends on what color you do your hair, purple or green. Do you have any more orange juice? We never get any at my house."

He takes her glass and heads for the fridge. "I think I would do purple."

"I know where your mind went today, during our chess game."

He refills the juice from the brightly colored bottle of *saft* and adds a little water from the tap, in case it's a long time before they can get more. He gives Lina her glass, then goes to a little tin on the counter, plucks out a piece of chocolate, and pops it in his mouth. It's the perfect balance of bitter and sweet—so much better than the Knusperflocken they have at the Konsum. He thinks it's probably from the West, with its label removed.

Having a grandfather who's a legendary Stasi agent does have its perks. (Franz's Opel, for one.) He's heard about the special grocery market inside Stasi headquarters, with all kinds of delicacies for the taking.

Lina takes a tiny sip of orange juice, savoring it. "You went over the wall again today, in your head."

Kurt eyes the chair across from her but can't bring himself to sit down. Nervous energy sends him pacing around the small wood-paneled living room. The events of the afternoon play like a videotape on fast forward. He goes to the window, then back to the tin for another chocolate. There is so much he wants to say to Lina and it's all competing for space, making him tongue-tied.

"My brother still won't talk about our parents!" he exclaims at last. "And he won't let me talk about them either. I'm not even allowed to speak their names."

"I know," Lina says softly.

He takes a deep breath. "Max and Hanna Muller," he says defiantly. By now Franz is many kilometers away, posted in one of those forbidding watch-towers, or patrolling the death strip. Kurt gestures around the living room. "Franz tore everything down. My mom used to have a keyboard and some sheet music—he even threw that away!" He points at the wall calendar. Erich Honecker glares down. "He put *that* up."

"I'm sorry," Lina says, setting the glass on the table. "Besides making really good spaetzle, he's a total jerk."

"You know what he told me after the Stasi took our parents away? He said they were foreign agents of the West and from now on we had to separate ourselves from the idea that they're our parents. *It's just us now, Kurt.* He said that if it wasn't for Grandpa Lothar using his power to save their lives and send them into exile, they would have been executed for treason. Because that's what happens to traitors."

Kurt thinks back to how his brother relished telling the story of the man with the false passport whom the guards shot at the checkpoint.

"Franz said it like he *wished* they had been killed!" Kurt knows he should keep his voice down so the nosy neighbors can't hear, but he can't help it. He turns his back to Lina, lifts the bottom of his shirt, and wipes his eyes with the fabric, leaving two wet stains.

"I'm sorry," Lina says again, quietly. She tucks a strand of hair behind her ear.

Kurt paces to the mango-colored sofa. He remembers sitting there while his mother read to him from books that Franz burned in a giant barrel in the weed-choked yard behind their apartment block. "It's not fair," he says, wincing at the whine in his voice. "If Franz loves it here so much, he can stay. I don't care. But why can't I go live in Kreuzberg? Why do they keep people here who don't want to be here and shoot them if they try to leave? It doesn't make any sense."

"It's like when we first started at the academy, do you remember?" Lina says. "I asked Frau Petrovsky why the knights move two spaces forward and one space to the side. It seemed so weird to me. And she just said *that's the way it is*. Like I was a total idiot for even asking."

"Yeah," Kurt says. "That's the way it is and don't question it. If you do, we'll kill you or arrest you or split up your family and send you away."

"My father hates the Westerners," Lina says. "He says they're American puppets who only care about money and Coca-Cola." She takes a sip of juice. "But my mom says we're all just Germans."

"Don't you want to find out which one is true?" Kurt glances nervously up at the photo of Honecker as if the stern head of state can actually hear what he's saying. At last, he sits at the table.

Lina puts down the glass. She peers at him with a blank yet focused expression. Kurt peers right back at her.

There is no board between them, no black and white pieces, but they are playing chess all the same. Kurt has to stifle a smile. This is why he and Lina are best friends. He knows her mind is churning as she sits in silence, studying him—several moves ahead, always.

"The Berlin Defense," she says at last. "A defensive game. A queen for a queen. What your brother said about the Swedish prime minister's visit. Suspending the shoot-to-kill order while he's here. It's their most dangerous tactic, taken off the board."

Kurt breaks into a grin. He can't help it. His heart is pounding with excitement. The two of them, best friends, plotting a glorious escape!

Checkmate, Franz.

But then Lina shakes her head. She doesn't smile. She looks as serious as Erich Honecker, up there on the wall. She leans forward and meets his eyes. "Listen to me, Kurt. You can't go."

Kurt notes that she didn't say *we* like he'd hoped she would. His heart sinks.

"Just because they won't shoot you doesn't mean they're going to let you scamper over the wall!"

"I know that, Lina. That's why we need a plan. The two of us together are smarter than any dumb grepo."

"It doesn't matter how smart we are! The wall's been up since our parents were kids. You think they haven't figured out how to stop people from crossing it by now?"

"There's always a weakness. It's like Frau Petrovsky says—"

"This isn't a chess game!"

"Everything's a chess game! Since we started at the academy, all I see is openings, middles, ends. The Italian Game, the Danish Gambit, all the different strategies running through my head all the time, nonstop, so fast I can hardly think straight."

Lina stands up. "Maybe you need a different hobby." She heads for the door. "This one's giving you crazy ideas."

"Where are you going?"

"Home."

"You didn't finish your orange juice."

Lina stops, returns to the table, and drains the glass. "Don't do it, Kurt. Please. I don't want you to go. Even if they don't kill you or arrest you, even if you make it—you'll be in the West, and I'll be in the East. Forever."

"So come with me," he says.

"*Your* parents are already in the West. *Mine* are still here! I can't just leave."

There's a long pause filled by the voice of the radio DJ listing upcoming concerts. Bands that will never be allowed to play in East Berlin.

"I'm sorry," Lina says. "I didn't mean it like that. I know none of this is easy."

"It's okay," Kurt says. The churning noise in his head slows down. Chess openings and defenses grind to a halt. He doesn't know what else to say.

Lina taps an odd rhythm on the table. She pokes him in the shoulder. He looks at the wall. Eventually, she leaves. He listens to her footsteps recede down the hall, then the stairs. There's the faint sound of her apartment door opening on the floor below. Then silence.

Kurt sits at the table for a long time, listening to the radio. Then he gets up and goes to the door of his brother's room, which used to belong to his parents. He turns on the light. It's neat, spotless, and organized. There's a small three-dimensional face gazing up from the desk: a white clay reproduction of Lenin's death mask. It was a birthday gift from their grandfather, and is Franz's prized possession. Kurt goes to the desk and opens a black three-ring binder. Franz's grepo training manual.

There, on page 37, is a diagram of a cross section of the wall. He studies it to make sure it matches the view from the sixth floor of the academy. He closes his eyes and transposes it with the little plots of kitchen gardens, laid out in squares like a chessboard.

So many places to hide until conditions are perfect. A shift change in the guard towers. A cloud passing over the moon.

He imagines creeping past the little sheds in the garden plots, taking one final look at East Berlin. City noise already drifting in from the West, car horns and music from the beer halls.

If Lina won't come, then you're going alone, he tells himself. But it doesn't feel right. He has to convince her. The two of them, escaping together, never coming back.

CHAPTER

At precisely nine thirty the following night, Franz switches on the television and settles into the sofa.

"Good evening, my dear ladies and gentlemen."

The man on the screen could be anyone's uncle, the one who gets invited to holiday dinner but makes people uncomfortable with his fierce political opinions. He reminds Kurt of some of the teachers at his school who insist on showing off how much they hate the West. His mouth is permanently curled into a slight sneer. He sports thick-lensed glasses and a graying beard. As he speaks, he hunches in his chair and looks straight into the camera.

"You have all, by now, heard the news that our courageous border guards have done their heroic duty once again."

"Border guards!" Franz nudges his brother with an elbow. "That's me!" Kurt looks up from his Digedags comic. He tries to ignore the man on television, but it's difficult when he's staring directly into the living room. And

Franz will just get angry if Kurt ignores the show completely and retreats into his room. So he sits on the sofa with his brother and tries his best to tune it out.

"Uh-huh," Kurt says, going back to the comic. But he's not paying much attention to the adventures of the Digedags either. His mind scrolls through the strategy of the Berlin Defense and overlays it with the map of the wall in Franz's grepo binder. It's all he can think about.

"This traitor was breaking the law, and by his sorry public display—his cowardly flight and refusal to stop when ordered—he has made himself a laughingstock."

The TV show is *Der Schwarze Kanal—The Black Channel*. Its host, Karl-Eduard von Schnitzler, has been the most famous figure of East German television since well before Kurt and Franz were born—since the earliest days of the wall, in fact, when it was just a temporary barrier.

"Why is it so difficult for people to understand that peace on earth cannot be achieved without protected borders?" Von Schnitzler acts incredulous that people could be so stupid. "The West calls us all kinds of childish names, even though we in the GDR—unlike, say, the Americans—have made peace a vital function of government! Our government exists in service of peace for all, not *money and riches for the few*!"

"Do you think he writes what he's going to say ahead of time?" Franz asks. "Or is he making it up as he goes along?"

"Dunno," Kurt says, trying not to shudder at the admiration in his brother's voice. Every single person he knows switches *off* the television as soon as *The Black Channel* comes on. To most East Germans—even loyal communists—von Schnitzler is a bit of a joke. Not to mention long-winded and boring.

Yet *The Black Channel* has somehow become Franz's favorite show. Another aspect of his brother that Kurt can't understand. He watches Franz out of the corner of his eye as he pretends to read the comic. Like yesterday, his brother is dressed in his full uniform, including his hat. He leans forward with his elbows on his knees, von Schnitzler's droning literally keeping him on the edge of his seat. Everything about him is neat and orderly—sideburns trimmed, face shaved and scrubbed. Not a single hair out of place.

"Ask yourselves," von Schnitzler urges, "what have I done for the cause of peace today? I am not a border guard, you might be saying. And to that I say, it matters not! All our workers are on the front lines of the fight for peace! And we must all be vigilant, in order to stamp out those who would threaten our noble cause, from within or without!"

"He means you," Franz says.

"Uh-huh."

The knock at the door—three sharp raps—startles them both.

Franz regards his brother with narrowed eyes. "Your little friend from downstairs?"

Kurt hasn't seen or spoken with Lina since she left yesterday. "I don't think so."

"Hmm." Franz gets up. "I'm not expecting anyone."

Of course you aren't, Kurt thinks. He can't remember the last time Franz had a friend over.

Franz approaches the door warily, as if it's going to burst open to reveal a rowdy crew of spiky-haired punks spoiling for a fight in their black-market Levi's. Kurt rolls his eyes.

Franz pauses with his hand on the doorknob and peers through the peephole. Then he pulls open the door with an excited flourish.

"Grandfather!" he exclaims. "It's great to see you. Come in, come in."

He stands aside, holding the door, as Lothar Muller enters the apartment.

Their grandfather's cane taps softly on the floor. For a big man with a pronounced limp, Lothar Muller moves with an imposing softness that always makes Kurt think of a sleepy yet sharp-eyed lion. His face, somehow both doughy and lined with deep creases, peeks out from a black wool cap. He tosses his hat on the table and leans his cane against the seat of a chair. The grip is carved into a thick knot of lacquered wood. Franz moves quickly behind their grandfather and tries to help with his overcoat.

"I've got it," Lothar says, "but take this." He offers a small white cardboard box he's wedged under his arm. Then he shrugs out of the coat and drapes it across the kitchen counter.

Franz holds the box with great reverence, a dumb smile plastered to his face.

"*Spritzkuchen,*" Lothar announces.

Kurt sets aside the comic at the mention of the fried, sugar-coated pastries. His mouth waters. He gets up from the sofa.

"For the boys at the wall," Lothar says. Kurt sits back down.

Franz grins. "I'm sure these won't last five minutes up in the tower. Hey, Grandfather, did you hear we shot another one?"

Lothar moves to sit down. Franz acts quickly and pulls out a chair for him. Lothar settles in and sighs. "What kind of question is that, Franz?"

"Right," Franz says. "Of course. You heard."

Lothar turns his head to regard von Schnitzler as the man drones away on the television screen. Kurt can't read his grandfather's face, but he thinks he sees a flicker of amusement. "How's Frau Petrovsky been treating you, Kurt?"

"Um," Kurt says. His guard goes up. He feels tingly, like someone is creeping up behind him, breathing lightly on his spine. He tries to give his grandfather the benefit of the doubt—when you've been a Stasi agent for several decades, it's probably difficult to ask people normal questions.

Questions that don't make them feel like they're being spied on at all times.

"She's . . . Russian," he says.

To his surprise, his grandfather laughs. "That she is. You know, her family was a noble one. Before the revolution did away with the entire concept of one family being better than another."

"I wish I could have seen it!" Franz exclaims. He takes off his uniform cap, runs a hand through his short hair. Lothar looks at him. He replaces the cap and clears his throat. "The revolution, I mean. Lenin in those early days." He shakes his head. "Nineteen sixteen. I can't even imagine it."

Kurt stares at his brother. Every day that passes, he feels like he understands Franz less and less. Where did this person come from, this alien in a grepo suit?

He feels, all at once, very lonely.

"Have you heard from our parents, Grandfather?" Kurt asks. *Your son and your daughter-in-law*, he thinks. If Lothar Muller was hurt by his only child's banishment, he has never betrayed any emotion about it one way or another. Kurt suspects there is something deeply wrong with this. The ability to go through life unscarred by terrible things. To keep moving forward as if nothing happened. His brother thinks Lothar Muller is the strongest person in East Berlin, but Kurt doesn't see it as strength. He's not sure what to call it.

"Kurt!" Franz says sharply. Then he turns to Lothar. "Sorry, Grandfather. He knows he's not to discuss them in this house. Or anywhere else."

Kurt's head begins to throb. His eyeballs feel tight in their sockets. He fights off the urge to act totally crazy. Tear the comic into shreds and dance wildly around the apartment, scattering torn paper like confetti.

"It's all right," Lothar says. "The answer is no. I have not."

"I told him to put them out of his mind," Franz says.

Their grandfather sighs. He glances at Honecker glowering down from the wall calendar. "The car needs petrol, Franz. And your shift starts in twenty minutes."

"Of course!" Franz springs to life, rushing to gather up his jacket and his keys and the box of spritzkuchen for his fellow grepos. "I'm sorry we didn't get a chance to talk! You know how much I love hearing your stories of the old days."

"Next time," Lothar assures him.

Half a minute later, his brother is gone. Off to work another shift on the wall, wishing someone—anyone!—would try to cross the border and give him an excuse to fire his rifle.

Lothar makes no attempt to move from his chair at the table. Kurt can't remember the last time he was alone with his grandfather. There is an infinite chessboard between them, a hundred thousand pieces, all dancing in and out of view. He doesn't know what to say. Lothar has always been a specter, breezing in and out of their lives, more shadow than man.

After a while, Kurt stands up. "Would you like some orange juice?"

A smile flickers on his grandfather's face. "Have you ever had fresh squeezed? With little bits of pulp?"

"No."

"Do you know where Florida is? In America?"

Kurt thinks for a moment. "The little tail at the bottom."

"Yes. The tail. That's where the best fresh-squeezed orange juice comes from. I'll get you some."

Kurt tries to figure out what his grandfather is getting at. How many moves ahead is he planning? "Thank you."

Lothar grips the head of his wooden cane and pushes himself to his feet. Kurt expects him to retrieve his coat and hat and head for the door. Instead, he makes his way over to the television. His left foot drags on the linoleum. At the TV he leans over and turns the volume up. *Way* up. Von Schnitzler's wheedling, smug voice is deafening. Kurt braces himself for some sort of

Stasi trick. His mind spins out of control. For a moment he thinks his grandfather's about to bludgeon him with his cane.

He watches, frozen to the floor, as Lothar goes to a sideboard lamp. He turns it off, lays it down on its side, and reaches up into its hollow base. On TV, von Schnitzler thunders on about protecting the East from Western spies *in the name of peace!* Lothar's entire forearm disappears inside the lamp. When it reappears, his hand clutches a small rectangular box, no bigger than a matchbook. Attached to the box are two wires, one blue and one orange, connected to a cylinder the size of a cigarette lighter.

Kurt's eyes go wide.

You don't have to be a Stasi agent to know a bugging device when you see one.

Lothar drops it on the floor. Without a word, he crosses the room to the kitchen counter. There, he turns the radio upside down, pulls a small collapsible tool from his pocket, and deftly removes a panel. A moment later, he produces an identical bug. He puts the radio back together, crosses the room once again, and drops the second device on the floor next to the first.

To Kurt's astonishment, he raises his heavy wooden cane and brings it down on the little pile of wire and plastic. *THUD.* Again and again, smashing the devices into bits. Satisfied, he extends the tip of his cane toward the TV and pokes a button. *Click.* Von Schnitzler goes quiet and the screen blinks off.

Kurt's mind spins frantically back through the past few weeks. All his dinners with Lina, everything they talked about in this very room—broadcast inside some listening booth at Stasi headquarters, where men in headphones dutifully transcribed his every traitorous word.

His heart pounds as he watches his grandfather retrieve his hat and coat. This man expelled his own son from the country—what will he do to Kurt?

Are there more Stasi agents waiting outside in a paddy wagon, ready to drag him off to the prison at Hohenschönhausen?

At the door, his grandfather turns back to regard him placidly. "I assure you, Kurt, you won't win a chess game against the Stasi. We own all the boards, and all the pieces, and we move them whether or not it's our turn." He hesitates. "Take some time to think it over. Don't be reckless. Contact me, and only me, if you still want to go."

"Go where?" he manages to say.

"Don't insult me, boy."

Kurt's mouth has gone dry. "Just call you?"

"Of course not." Lothar Muller raises his cane and points at a slip of paper on the table. Kurt hadn't seen him leave it there. "Commit it to memory, then burn it."

With that, he's gone. No encouragement, no warning, no goodbye. Just gone, his cane tap-tap-tapping down the stairs at the end of the hallway.

Kurt stands rooted to the floor in a kind of numb panic. He doesn't understand what just happened. Surely it's a trap. There's no way Lothar Muller, Stasi hero, just offered to help him escape over the wall.

Right?

Stasi Headquarters
The House of a Thousand Eyes

The chalkboard on the wall of the windowless classroom says SIGNALS FOR OBSERVATION.

Lothar Muller stands at the head of the class in full uniform—he is *Major Lothar Muller* when he teaches the enlisted men and women. His cane leans against the rim of the chalkboard. Before him, nineteen young men and six young women sit in folding metal chairs with small desks attached to their arms. Each student sits poised with pen and open notebook. The heat in the room is stifling. The radiator clicks and pops.

Lothar pulls a handkerchief from his back pocket and briefly lifts it to his nose. Then he looks around the room. Seven hands shoot up. He calls on an eager young woman by pointing at her. Petra or Ilse or something. These days—these endless, gray-tinted days—all his students blur together.

"The signal handkerchief to nose means *watch out*," she says, "the subject under surveillance is coming your way."

"Correct."

He waits a moment as the class takes notes. When most of the students have returned to watching him intently, he places his right palm on his stomach. Eleven hands this time. He calls on a hawkish man in the back. He doesn't even bother guessing at his name.

"The subject is standing still!" The student's voice booms as if he's onstage, trying to reach the audience in the back of the theater.

Muller nods. "Good."

He scans the fresh faces arrayed in their sad little desks, all chipped paint and scratches. There had been a time when he'd been one of them—a time before the wall, even. When the borders were still technically open. When his own excitement for the future of the Party and the State—and the part he was to play in it all—could barely be contained. There had been a sense, once, of history as a series of locked doors, and his life a journey toward finding the keys.

As his mind wanders back through the decades, he continues to teach by sheer reflex. The class laughs at a joke he can't even remember making.

"Now," he says, "who can demonstrate to the class the signal for *cover threatened, terminate observation?*"

"I'll give it a shot, Major." A man is standing in the door to the classroom. Muller has no idea how long he's been watching the lessons.

"Colonel Weber!" Muller says, beckoning the man into the room. "We would be honored."

Any trace of the slightly nervous young man his former assistant Klaus used to be has been worn away by his rise through the Stasi ranks. Klaus has reached the level three rungs above Muller himself, who's been holding steady at major for many years now. Klaus's fine hair, once like spun gold, has gone prematurely gray. His smooth boyish face has acquired the lines of a man twice his age. He strides with purpose to the head of the class. Then, with theatrical grace, Klaus goes down on one knee, unties and reties a shoelace.

He stands up and takes a bow. There is a smattering of applause. The students have never been visited by such a high-ranking member of the Stasi, and Muller knows they will be unsure how to react.

Klaus—Colonel Weber, Muller reminds himself for the millionth time—tries to put them at ease with a casual, lopsided grin. "You're too kind," he says. Some of the students look at him in awe. It's not every day that a Stasi colonel comes to joke around with your class.

"I'm sorry to interrupt, comrades," Klaus says, "but I have some urgent business with my old friend the major here." He shoots Muller an apologetic glance. "So"—he shrugs—"class dismissed?"

Muller nods. He addresses his students. "I expect you all to be well versed in Directive 1/79 by the next time I see you. Dismissed."

The students file out, a few of them sneaking quick glances back at the visiting colonel. Klaus trails the last student to the door and closes it behind her.

"On the conversion of and collaboration with informers," Klaus says.

"You've correctly identified 1/79," Muller says. "Gold star, as they say in America."

"How's this latest crop of up-and-comers?" Klaus sits down in an empty chair and taps a fingertip against the desktop.

Muller turns and erases the words on the board. "Same as the last, and the one before that." Chalk dust billows. Muller coughs. "How is your family?"

"Gisela's just started her second term at Humboldt."

"Good, good. And you, Klaus?" He makes his way over to his own desk and sits down in his well-worn chair. "What's buzzing over at the Administration for Security of Heavy Industry?"

"They still haven't given me that house in Potsdam, if that's what you're getting at."

Muller shrugs. "We pretend to work—"

"—and they pretend to pay us." Klaus smiles thinly at the old joke. He glances at the wall clock, then fixes his gaze on Muller.

"Urgent business," Muller reminds him. "Best get to it."

"Yes." Klaus looks like he's just experienced a stomach pain. "It's come to my attention that the electronic surveillance of Kurt and Franz Muller was abruptly terminated."

"I didn't realize my grandsons were of such high importance to the Heavy Industry department."

Klaus's expression turns cold. *That was quick,* Muller thinks as he studies his former protégé. *Klaus is sticking his neck out and in no mood for sarcasm.*

Klaus once again glances at the wall clock. He lowers his voice. "Perhaps the devices malfunctioned. Or perhaps the room was rearranged. As you know better than anyone, there could be many reasons for the bugs' sudden failure."

"These things do happen."

Klaus taps a finger on the desktop. A swing rhythm, one-two, one-two. "Remember what you told me at the beginning of the Dietrich operation, back in—what was it?"

"Nineteen sixty-one. Refresh my memory."

"*Psychology*, you told me, back when I was young and nervous and overly sensitive. *Emotion, opinion*—we can't deny ourselves these things. We're human, after all. But simply let them float like wine corks on an ocean of the facts." Another thin, brittle smile. "I never lost sight of this lesson." He rises from the desk. "You, on the other hand . . . Well, who can say?"

The rest is unspoken. *There's a reason I'm a colonel and you've been stuck at major for fifteen years.*

"I'm grateful for all that you've taught me, and done for me, over the years," Klaus says. "That's why I'm keeping you informed, so you can correct the problem over at your grandsons' apartment, before more eyes are assigned to the file."

Muller sighs wearily. "All right. Thank you, Klaus."

Klaus had clearly been expecting a sharp-tongued retort or at least some assertiveness. Muller sees disgust pass across the colonel's face. He can't blame the man. He's disgusted with himself too.

"Listen to me, Lothar. If that grandson of yours ends up in the West, you will be held personally responsible. I don't have to tell you what that means. Or what will happen to you."

With that, the colonel turns smartly on his heel and leaves Muller alone in the classroom. He finds that he's still holding the eraser and sets it down on his desk. He stares at it for a moment. *Nineteen sixty-one*, he thinks. With a single finger he pushes the eraser across the chipped metal surface—a train on the tracks, gathering steam, until it plunges off the edge.

DECEMBER 22, 1961

"Hallo, Schneider."

It is three o'clock in the morning. This voice on the other end—this "Frau Schneider"—doesn't sound weary, or tired, or annoyed. To Marta, she sounds like she always does. Like she's been sitting by the phone. Like answering strange calls is her job. For all Marta knows, it is.

"Hallo." Marta considers them to be on friendlier, more personal terms now. "This is the ghost of Christmas past." She stands in the darkened kitchen, bare feet on the frozen linoleum, keeping her voice low.

"How are things in Berlin?" Frau Schneider says.

Marta closes her eyes, remembers her latest assignment from Harry. She's still not allowed to write anything down. She doesn't want to mess up the order of the code words. "We had some more snow. Not as bad as Dresden."

Outside on Bernauer Strasse, a dog barks. The grepos have installed dog runs along certain sections of the border fence—big German shepherds chained to long crossbars, giving them space to roam. And hunt. And snap at anyone who comes too close. At night, she can hear their lonely cries.

Poor pups must be freezing. She hopes the grepos dress them in coats.

"I hope the weather didn't change your plans."

"No," Marta says, "everything's on schedule. As long as there's a little bit of green."

"There's plenty."

"That's great!" Marta says, wincing. Too loud. The walls here are very thin.

Frau Schneider seems to hesitate. When she resumes speaking, there's something different about her voice. "You know," she says, "I once lost some-one I loved who tried to leave and never came back."

Marta freezes. What does Frau Schneider know about her?

"I'm sorry," Marta says.

"It's all right." There's a pause. In the living room, Penelope whines in her sleep. The kitchen is bathed in pale blue light from a streetlamp outside. Everything has an underwater glow—the toaster, the Riga clock, the table. "It does get better, you know. We find ways to keep going. This is one of them."

Marta doesn't need to ask what Frau Schneider means by *this*. She under-stands. Since the morning "out back" at her cousin Harry's, when she was brought into the escape plan, Marta hasn't needed to chop the day up into little snippets of time. No more *okay*s. Just regular days defined by a goal. Something to be done in Stefan's memory—something important, and daring.

"Thank you," Marta says. "I hope I get to meet you someday."

Suddenly, the kitchen light comes on. Marta slams the phone down into its cradle and opens the refrigerator door. Her heart pounds as she leans into the fridge, pretending to rummage.

"Marta." Her father's voice. She grabs a plastic container, shuts the refrigerator door, takes a moment to compose herself, and turns.

Her father is standing in the doorway. He's wearing his bathrobe and rubbing his eyes. "It's three in the morning," he says. "Who were you talking to?"

"Nobody!" Marta says brightly. "I was just getting a snack." She holds up the container to find that it's little pieces of chicken liver for Penelope. She sets it down on the table.

Her father stifles a yawn, then steps into the kitchen. Marta braces herself for some kind of admonishment. *Tell me the truth*, or at the very least, *get back to bed*. But he walks right past her to the chalkboard, where he pauses to look at the tally.

"Stefan never told us he was planning to swim the harbor before he left that night," he says.

"I know," Marta says. "He didn't tell me either."

Her father runs a finger down the eighth tally mark, erasing it from the board. Then he picks up the chalk and redraws it, tracing the ghostly remains of the line. "Maybe, if he'd spoken to us about it, we could have talked him out of it. I think about that every day, you know. If there was something I missed, something I could have said. Some way I could have made him change his mind." He turns around and Marta's breath catches in her throat. He looks exactly like he did at Stefan's memorial. Like he desperately wants to ask a question but doesn't know the words, or who he's supposed to say them to. He tries to give her a smile. Then he steps forward and wraps her up in a hug.

"Are you two having a party?" Her father lets her go as her mother enters the kitchen, nightgown swishing. "This is just how I wanted to spend my night off, thank you." She shivers. "It's freezing in here."

She eyes the chicken liver on the table and raises an eyebrow. "Midnight snack?"

"Marta was just about to tell me who she was talking to on the phone," her father explains.

Her mother frowns. "Marta, what's going on?"

"I'm sorry I woke you up," she says quietly. Helmut's face flashes in her mind, glaring at her while Harry explains that she can't tell anyone about her assignments. Not even her parents. *Especially* not her parents. The plan depends on it.

Her father fills the kettle with water but leaves it in the sink. Then he opens a cupboard and stares at a stack of plates.

"*What* is going on with you lately?" her mother says. Penelope, the last one to wake, pads over to the doorway and stops to regard everyone for a moment. The puppy cocks her little head—how strange, this family gathered in the kitchen during sleep time. Then she heads to her dish and slurps water.

"Nothing," Marta says.

Her father slams the cupboard shut with a *BANG*. "That's what Stefan told us too!" His voice is startlingly loud in the predawn silence.

"*Pieter!*" her mother says. "You'll wake the neighborhood."

Marta's eyes go wide. Her father never yells. Never raises his voice. With his palm still on the cupboard door, he leans to press his forehead against the back of his hand and closes his eyes. "I'm sorry," he says softly.

"Sit." Her mother points to a chair. Marta sits at the table. Her mother takes a seat across from her. "Pieter, please join us," she says. After a moment, her father sits down too. Next to the container of chicken liver, a white ceramic vase holds brittle, decaying flowers left over from an autumn walk in the park. Bits of crinkly old petals surround the vase.

"I work nights," Alma says matter-of-factly. "It's the job I was given by the labor exchange. There's nothing I can do about it. You"—she looks at Marta—"have school. You"—she looks at Marta's father—"sleep whenever you're not at work. Or else you're wandering around, in your own head, somewhere far away." She pauses. "All these separate things are no one's fault, not really—but that doesn't mean we can't work on being closer. Stefan is gone, but we are still a family. I think it's time we acted like one again, starting right now. Beginning with you, Marta."

Marta withers under her mother's Teacher Look.

"Why were you making a phone call at three in the morning?"

"Um," Marta says. Helmut's face looms in her mind. And Harry, swearing her to secrecy, imploring her to keep quiet about her role in the grand plan. Her parents would be extremely angry to know that he's involved her. Once they're safely in the West, Marta has imagined letting her parents in on her secret role in the escape. With the whole family in West Berlin, they might be still be angry, but they will have to admit that it was worth it.

"Marta," her father says. "This sorry excuse for a country runs on secrets. This family can't, or we're no better than the petty little Ulbrichts in charge. It's that simple."

"She calls herself Schneider!" Marta blurts out. "I don't think that's her real name, but I don't know. Please don't be mad."

"Okay," her mother says, visibly anxious. "How do you know this Schneider? What were you talking to her about in the middle of the night?"

"*Stallgeruch,*" her father mutters. Marta has heard the term before—the smell of the pigsty.

The stink of suspicion, the stench of the Stasi.

Marta shakes her head. "She's not Stasi."

Her mother exhales. "You don't know that. You can never know that."

"She's somebody who works with Harry!"

Her father considers this. "This woman is a train conductor?"

"No," Marta says. "I don't think so. She's somebody who's helping with the plan."

Her parents glance at each other. "What plan?" her mother says. "What has your cousin gotten you into now?"

Marta glances from her mother to her father. They're both waiting expectantly for her to explain what's going on.

Marta is confused. "*The* plan," she says. Surely Harry has told them about it? They're all supposed to be coming! She lowers her voice. "Escaping to the West. You, me, Harry, and Monika, and all the kids . . . you know. The plan."

There's a long pause. Outside, a dog barks twice, short and sharp. "No," her mother says at last. "We don't know."

Marta doesn't understand. "Yes, you do," she insists. "Harry said he's taking all of us. He just didn't want you to know I was making the calls because he knew you'd be mad. But he told you about the plan. He must have!"

"Well, Harry's right about one thing," her father says. "We are mad." Then he turns to her mother. "That idiot is going to get us all killed." He rises from the table with enough force to topple his chair and storms into the living room.

"Where are you going?" her mother calls after him, forgetting to be quiet.

"To have a little talk with Harry."

Alma Dietrich throws up her hands. "Pieter, it's the middle of the night."

"I don't care." He appears in the doorway, putting his coat on over his bathrobe. "We just lost Stefan," he says fiercely. "Does he want us to lose Marta too? What is he thinking, getting her involved in some crazy scheme of his?"

Some crazy scheme. It dawns on Marta—too late—that her parents really, truly, have no idea what she's talking about. "Harry didn't tell you about the plan?"

"No," her mother says. "He did not."

Her father comes back into the kitchen, hands her mother a pair of fuzzy slippers, and sits back down at the table with his coat on. "What exactly did Harry tell you to do?"

She tells her parents about the phone calls to "Schneider," about the code words she's supposed to work into the conversation.

As she speaks, her mother presses her lips together and her father goes pale.

"The man is insane," he says when she's finished. "He has some kind of death wish and he's going to drag us all with him!"

At the words *death wish*, Marta feels a hot, burning lump in her throat. She wishes she could go back to the day she brought pork schnitzel to her cousin's house. Instead of going out back to overhear Harry and Helmut talking about their escape plan, she could have just stayed inside and helped Monika with the children.

"I was just trying to help us get to a better place." Her voice cracks. Then the words tumble out. "I hate it here! Everything's a lie. They lied about Stefan in the paper. They killed him and they lied about it!" She turns to her father, who is sitting with one hand squeezing the other. "You said so yourself. This sorry excuse for a country is all about secrets and lies, and grepos and guns and walls."

Her father gets up, paces over to the chalkboard. He knocks on it once with his fist, then puts his hands on his hips and stares at the wall, shaking his head.

"Pieter, please sit down," her mother says. "You're making me nervous."

"This is my fault too," her father says without turning around.

"No, Papa," Marta says.

He puts a hand on his head and scratches at his scalp. "I haven't been honest either."

"It seems like we need to have more family meetings," her mother says.

"I've been visiting Stefan," he says. "Alone, I mean." He comes back to the table, eyes downcast. "At the cemetery."

Something clicks in the back of Marta's mind. That strange evening, a few weeks ago, after her mother left for the factory.

"Stamp collecting," she says. "In a suit."

Her mother slaps her palms flat on the table. "I think I need to go back to bed. *Stamp collecting?*"

Her father reaches across the table to take her mother's hand in his. "That memorial they *allowed* us to have for Stefan was a joke. He deserves better. I want him to know he's not alone." He shrugs. "I don't know. I couldn't help it. I have to mourn him."

"Without us," her mother says quietly.

"I'm sorry," he says.

Her mother moves aside the vase and takes Marta's hand, so they're all connected in the center of the table like spokes of a wheel. "All right," she says. "This is how it is from now on. No more secrets, no more living inside our own heads. We do things together, as a family, or not at all. We honor Stefan that way."

"I don't want to live in the East anymore," Marta says. "It feels wrong here without him."

Her father wipes his eyes with the sleeve of his robe. "We have to make the best of it."

"I know this is hard," her mother says, "but you have to understand, we can't just up and leave—not now. The Stasi have been watching us closely ever since they shot Stefan. Remember those men who paid us a visit?"

Marta nods. *Candy-cane man!* It finally clicks. He'd been dressed in a suit, and he didn't have the shaggy-haired beatnik look, but he was one of the men who came over unannounced after Stefan's memorial.

"Listen to me, Marta," her mother continues. "You're not to see Harry or speak with him, not until we tell you it's safe. Understand?"

"Yes," she says.

"Our phones are probably tapped," her father says. Marta's heart sinks. She imagines a smoky room full of Stasi goons, all of them listening to her calls with Frau Schneider.

Her father leans forward and lowers his voice. "For all we know, they bugged the apartment too."

Stallgeruch, Marta thinks. The smell of the pigsty. The stink of suspicion and fear and mistrust.

Since last night—or, she supposes, early this morning, when her parents woke up to confront her—she hasn't been able to get the lingering stench out of her nostrils. It floats through the halls and classrooms of her school as she tries to stay awake while Frau Vandenburg drones on and on. It's a bad smell—fear and sweat and dirty old socks and smoke. She can't believe she didn't notice it before, hanging over all of East Berlin.

The smell of the secret police.

It surrounds her now as she hurries down the cobbled streets south of the Mauerpark. The spire of the Zionskirche pokes up through the spindly, leafless trees. Midafternoon and it's already getting dark. Her breath steams in the cold air. Every face on the street leers at her from beneath wool hats and bundled scarves. Every neighbor an informer.

Sitting at the kitchen table with her parents, it had been easy to agree with them—no more escape plan, no more contact with her cousin, no more secrets. But now, after dragging herself through an entire day at school on no sleep, a sense of recklessness has taken over.

Why didn't Harry tell her parents about the plan if they're all supposed to be coming with him? Why did he ask her to make secret phone calls if their phones might be tapped?

Is it all some sort of trick? Is he leaving without them? Is he leaving at all?

Is he Stasi himself?

Maybe it really was Harry's idea to have Gerhard join the Young Pioneers.

Her head swims. She needs to sleep. But her legs carry her south, away from Bernauer Strasse, away from home. Toward what she hopes will be some answers.

After today, she promises herself, she'll abide by her parents' rules. No contact with her cousin. No secrets.

She comes to a nondescript door. A window is covered in white lace curtains, behind which yellow light struggles mightily against the winter gloom. She was only ever inside this place once, last summer, for Harry and Monika's anniversary party. But she never forgot the running joke between her parents—only Harry would throw an anniversary bash at the neighborhood *kneipe*, the pub where he hangs out with his railroad comrades.

If you want to find Harry Dietrich after his shift on the DR, you go to the kneipe.

She pauses just outside, rehearsing what she's going to say. The words swim in the soupy fog of a sleepless night. She decides she's just going to wing it and pushes open the door.

A wave of hot air hits her. The entire place is lined with dark wood. A fire crackles in a small hearth. The wall is cluttered with dusty photographs and ancient portraits. It's a bit like stepping into an old relative's cozy apartment, one with lots of cats. The drinkers—all men—are huddled around scarred tables and jammed side by side at the bar. They all look up at once at the unlikely sight of the twelve-year-old girl barging into their sacred space.

At the bar, Harry turns to look over his shoulder. He doesn't seem happy to see her. The broad-backed man next to him turns and looks even less happy, glowering at her with his one good eye. She hasn't seen Helmut since that day in the air shaft behind Harry's apartment, and she has forgotten how dangerous his scowl looks.

She tries to ignore the stares. "I need to talk to you," she says to her cousin.

A low murmur sweeps through the crowd. A few snickers. Some of the men smirk. "You're in trouble now, Harry," someone says.

A bald man in shirtsleeves and red suspenders steps out from behind the bar. "You'll have to clear out," he says gruffly, pointing to the door behind her. "I can't have kids in here."

"Easy, Otto," Harry says, getting up out of his seat. "I'll take her outside."

Harry meets Marta's eyes and nods at the door. She heads back out. Helmut follows wordlessly, buttoning his overcoat.

On the street, Harry looks from left to right. "Come on," he says, ducking down the narrow alleyway next to the kneipe. Marta steps over a wet gray blob she doesn't want to examine closely. Outside the pub's back door is an overflowing barrel of trash.

She can't escape the bad smells of East Berlin today.

"I notice you don't come bearing pork schnitzel this time," Harry says. "I have to check with some of the others, but that *might* affect your favorite cousin status moving forward. So! To what do I owe the pleasure? By the way, did you see the look on old Otto's face when you walked in? It was like you just stormed the castle keep."

"Stupid," Helmut says, "you coming here to see us. Very stupid." He sips from the huge mug he brought outside with him.

"You lied to me," she says, ignoring the big man.

Harry seems taken aback. "I would never lie to you, Marta. I meant every word I said. The plan is in motion."

"You said we were all going to the West. You said you were taking all of us. My parents didn't even know anything about it!"

Harry's smile fades. "I told you not to talk to anyone about what you're doing!"

"They caught me on the phone last night, I didn't have a choice. And anyway, I don't even *know* what I'm doing! Why am I even calling this Schneider person and saying these things? What do they mean?"

"Too many questions," Helmut says.

Harry takes a breath. "What my esteemed colleague is trying to say is this: We are compartmentalized. Do you understand what the word means?"

"Like train compartments?"

"Yes. Like train compartments. Little boxes that keep people completely separate. That way the man with the stinky cigar doesn't know anything about the lady with the babies, and she doesn't know anything about the rowdy soldiers next to her. And none of them know anything about the conductor who didn't get the pork schnitzel he loves so much. They're all traveling on the same train but they never see one another. In our case, it's information that's kept separate."

"Or at least it was till you screwed up the job we gave you," Helmut says.

"It wasn't my fault!" Marta says, fighting tears. She's more tired than she's ever been, and her nerves are shredded, yet she also feels overly alert. It's a strange combination and it makes her want to cry and stamp her feet in the muck of the alley.

"Helmut," Harry says without looking at him. "Go back inside and order me a schnapps."

Helmut doesn't move. He stares Marta down with his good eye. She thinks of the time the Digedags stole that pirate treasure in the South Pacific. The smell of rotten fruit drifts past.

Harry sighs. "All right. No schnapps. Marta, what Helmut is so diplomatically trying to say is, everybody involved in this plan has a certain role, and each role is kept separate from the others, like assembly jobs in a factory. Nobody knows exactly what anybody else is doing, but—"

"You just explained this," Marta says.

Helmut snorts and sips from his mug.

"The whole point," Harry says, getting irritated, "is to keep the Stasi from finding out about the plan *as a whole*. So no one person knows the details of the entire thing. Everybody gets bits and pieces."

"That way they can't torture it out of you," Helmut chimes in.

Marta considers this. She fights through the fog in her head like the Digedags hacking away at the Amazon jungle with their cartoon machetes. Then she shakes her head. *Stupid Digedags.*

"That makes sense, I guess," she says. "Except my parents didn't get a little piece of the plan. They didn't get anything at all."

"The Stasi are too close to your parents," Harry explains. "Ever since Stefan . . ." He trails off. Marta understands. Ever since her brother was killed trying to swim to West Berlin, the Stasi have had a close eye on her family. "So," Harry says, "I can't bring Alma and Pieter in until the very last moment, just before we go, in the first minutes of Christmas Eve. We'll just have to spring it on them."

"Christmas Eve!" Marta is stunned. "That's the day after tomorrow!"

"It is indeed, Favorite Cousin," Harry says. As if attached to a string, his head turns along with Helmut's as a man stops in the entrance of the alley. His dark outline is frozen there for a moment, and then he's gone.

"I have to tell you something bad," she says.

"Everything's bad right now," Harry says. "We just keep chasing the idea that one day there will be something good in store for us. So tell me."

"My father said he thinks our phone might be tapped. So the Stasi could have heard everything I said to Frau Schneider. All the code words. I'm sorry, Harry. I didn't know."

She glances at Helmut, bracing herself for the man's furious anger.

Nothing.

She turns to Harry. He doesn't seem upset, or horrified, or even disappointed. He glances at Helmut, who shrugs. Then he puts a gentle hand on Marta's shoulder.

"Your phone is definitely being tapped," he tells her.

Marta blinks. His words get lost in the fog inside her head. "What?"

"The Stasi heard you loud and clear," Helmut says. "Every word. That was your job."

Marta shakes her head. "No."

"I'm afraid so," Harry says. He tries on a reassuring smile. "This was your role. You fed them code words we picked out. It was all misdirection, Marta. A great big fake-out for our friends in the secret police. Make them think we'll be on the green line out of Dresden on Christmas Day."

She twists away from him and steps back toward the mouth of the alley. "So you did lie to me!"

"No," Harry says.

"We *used* you, kid," Helmut says. "There's a difference. Don't take it personally."

Harry strides forward and takes her roughly by the arm. Marta gasps. All her cousin's chatty, loopy kindness has been squeezed out of him.

"I'm sorry, Marta, but this isn't a game. You're in it now, same as us. Be at the Bernauer Strasse U-Bahn station platform at one minute after midnight on Christmas Eve. That means late tomorrow night, you leave. Get your parents there too, any way you can."

She wrenches herself away from him, twisting her body so hard she nearly flings herself down into the gray slop beneath her feet.

Trust. What a joke.

At the mouth of the alley, her feet skid on the slick cobblestones and she flails to stay upright. She runs north, toward the park, toward home. Her cousin's face flashes through her mind—all the family dinners and parties, all his jokes and stories. And her last glimpse of him, in the dim alleyway, face as hard and unyielding as Helmut's. Who is he, really?

Lost in thought, bone-weary, she rounds the corner onto Bernauer Strasse. The wall looms at the edge of her vision—

And something hits her in the stomach. Her breath whooshes out of her. The cold ground comes up fast. A crumpled wrapper and a slushy boot print are all she can see.

"My goodness!" A hand reaches down to help her up. "Where are we rushing off to in such a hurry?"

The man looming over her pops a candy cane into his mouth.

Marta ignores the helping hand and pushes herself up to her feet.

"Nowhere," she mutters. Inside, she's screaming. Why couldn't she just be home, in her warm bed, surrounded by cooking smells while Penelope nuzzles her face? She feels like she's trapped in a nightmare, the kind where you run and run but the hallway keeps getting longer, stretching out into infinity.

She brushes bits of dirty slush off her jacket and walks right past the man, up Bernauer Strasse.

A moment later, he falls in beside her. Somehow, he seems to be ambling along without effort, even as she quickens her pace. He's wreathed in sweet peppermint, but it might as well be stallgeruch.

Marta knows what this man is.

"Why don't I walk you home," he says. It doesn't sound like a question or a friendly offer.

Marta doesn't say anything. She doesn't look at him. Out of the corner of her eye she watches as he spins the candy cane in his front teeth, working it into a spiraling point.

They pass Harry and Monika's building, where she saw this very man loitering on the stoop the day she got sucked into this nightmare world.

She quickens her pace.

"Are you familiar with Hohenschönhausen?" This *does* sound like a question, but he keeps talking before she can answer. "It has many other names. Some refer to it as a prison, but I like to think of it as a hotel for citizens of our state who believe they'd be more comfortable elsewhere. In the West, perhaps."

A Trabant clatters past them, windows fogged. She's only three blocks from home. She keeps her eyes glued to the sidewalk ahead.

"It's not very far from here, you know. Just east of the Volkspark. We could walk there, if we wanted to. Of course, guests receive a ride from us, free of charge, in one of our official vehicles."

He gestures at the wall that slices her street in half. "Your first sight of it wouldn't be so different from our Anti-Fascist Protection Barrier here. But then you'd pass the steel entry gates, into the yard. It looks like it might be a decent place to take some air and get some exercise, but there will be no one out and about. And when you enter the building in the center of that yard, you still won't see any of the other guests. In fact, for the entire duration of your stay, you'll *never* see another guest. We take isolation very seriously. It gives our guests ample room to reflect."

One of the German shepherds in the dog run sprints along the other side of the fence. His chain slides along the pole.

"Down a staircase into the basement of this building," the man continues, "is where we welcome our most honored guests. Some of our therapeutic treatments include small concrete rooms where the lights never do seem to come on. These rooms are quite soundproof, I assure you. Many of our honored guests have been there for years. In fact, some enjoy it so much that they're never leaving!"

Up ahead, her apartment block comes into view. Marta moves as fast as she can without breaking into a run. Her neighbor Herr Schmidt walks up the front steps, laden with groceries.

"You know," muses the candy-cane man at her side, "Herr Schmidt is quite the gardener. His rhododendrons are exceptional."

They are nearly at the stoop now. Marta wonders with mounting horror if the man will follow her inside the building. "Well, we're almost there. Oh," he says, as if he just remembered something, "we've got some very nice guest rooms picked out for your parents. In fact, two of our finest rooms have recently become available."

Marta's feet are blocks of lead. She fights to keep moving.

"Tell me about the train," he demands. "Tell me everything I need to know about your little plan, and I'll cancel Pieter and Alma's reservation at Hohenschönhausen. Otherwise, I'll be seeing them very soon."

She bounds up the steps to the front door.

"Check your pocket, Marta!" the man calls after her. "Tell me what I need to know. Time is running out."

She fumbles with her keys. Behind her, the man walks away, whistling, boots crunching slush. She finally gets the key in the lock.

Once inside, she slams the door behind her and leans against it, breathing hard. She reaches into her coat pockets. Her right hand brushes a stiff piece of paper. She pulls it out to find a small rectangular card. Written in neat block letters is a phone number, followed by a name: *Lothar*.

Somehow, he slipped the card into her pocket without her noticing.

In a daze, she stares at the letters and numbers. The loops of the *o* and the *a* take the shape of two dark prison cells waiting to swallow her parents up unless she becomes the kind of person who betrayed her brother.

An informer.

Marta dreams of drowning.

She is with Stefan underneath Humboldt Harbor's train bridge. He is somewhere nearby—she can feel the vibrations of the cold, dark water. It's impossible to tell which way is up. Lights from the bridge shimmer on the surface, but there are lights below her too, at the bottom of the harbor, as if she's trapped between mirrors. She cries out and water rushes into her lungs.

All at once she bumps into something that floats up from the depths. Her brother's face, as white-gray as the sky over Berlin. He opens his mouth and his voice is strange. Her name comes out and floats away.

"Marta."

He disappears. The lights go out. Only her name remains.

"Marta!"

She opens her eyes.

"*Willkommen*, Marta Dietrich." Frau Vandenburg stands before the class, peering at Marta from behind thick glasses that magnify her eyes. Her dark hair is held firmly in place by a spray that makes it look like a shiny helmet. "Nice of you to join us."

The class titters. Frau Vandenburg holds up a single finger and the noise dies away. Behind her on the chalkboard are the names of eight countries: Albania, Bulgaria, Czechoslovakia, East Germany, Hungary, Poland, Romania, Soviet Union.

"You were about to tell us what these nations have in common," she says.

"Um," Marta says, "I was?" She rubs her eyes. Last night, all she wanted to do was fall into a deep sleep, but every time she started to drift off, Lothar's voice jolted her awake.

Tell me what I need to know.

The card is in her pocket. The card with the phone number. It burns a rectangular imprint into her thigh. It whispers of the prison cells at Hohenschönhausen. Dark, cold, empty.

Waiting for her parents.

She wants to close her eyes and go back to sleep for days.

"Marta Dietrich!" Frau Vandenburg, exasperated, approaches Marta's desk. The air goes out of the room as her classmates hold their breath. "You are privileged to live in a *workers' paradise*. Which remains a paradise only so far as its citizens are *working*. Do you want to grow up to be a parasite?"

"No, Frau Vandenburg," she says.

"Good. Parasites belong in the West. Now, take a look at the board and answer my question."

Tell me what I need to know.

Marta's sleepy eyes sweep across the names of the familiar countries. The boy in front of her swivels in his seat to stare her down. He is smirking, waiting for her to fail.

"They're all socialist nations," Marta says. "And members of the Warsaw Pact."

The boy's smirk vanishes. He gives her a dirty look, then turns back around.

"Correct," Frau Vandenburg says. "And what is the purpose of the Warsaw Pact?"

Suddenly, she gets that elevator-drop feeling in her stomach. There is so much on her mind, so much *weight*, that it feels like the stress of it all is bouncing around inside her. She's hungry one second, full the next. Jumpy one second, tired the next.

"A treaty of friendship for defense against the United States and the other imperialist countries of NATO."

"Thank you."

Marta knows she has to make up her mind.

Inform on her cousin. Betray the escape plan. Save her parents from prison.

Or take her chances with Harry and beg her parents to go West. Hope they can all somehow slip through Lothar's fingers.

Time is running out.

"Marta!" She blinks to find that her classmates are on their feet, gathering up their books. Frau Vandenburg has been trying to get her attention again. The other students shuffle from the classroom, leaving Marta alone at her desk. "You may go to lunch now," the teacher says. "And when we resume lessons this afternoon, I expect you to be fully present. Do you understand?"

Marta gets up. "Yes, Frau Vandenburg."

Out in the hall, the chatter of lunch-bound kids washes over her. Friends pass nearly unnoticed. She finds herself standing still in the middle of a traffic stream as it parts to flow around her like minnows.

Die Elritze. The Minnow. That's what Stefan called his best friend, Johann. The boy he was with on the night of his death.

She closes her eyes. Her brother's pale face floats across the backs of her eyelids. Dark as the cells in the basement of the Stasi prison. Her parents' future home.

She imagines sneaking off to one of the public telephones across the street from her school. Nobody would be there. Nobody uses the public phones because everybody knows the Stasi listen to them. But in this case, it wouldn't matter—she'd be calling the Stasi anyway.

No. There is nothing worse than being an informer. But is it okay when you're trying to save your family?

Maybe that's what every informer thinks: *I'm doing this for a good reason. I'm not as bad as the others.*

I have no choice.

"Asleep on your feet?"

She opens her eyes to find Gerhard standing there in his Young Pioneers uniform. She finds it hard to believe anybody would choose to wear a stupid white collared shirt with a red necktie *on purpose*, but she sees them every day at school, strutting around the halls and the cafeteria. There are six of them here now, blocking traffic in the hall.

"Hi, Gerhard," she says. Her eyes scan his fellow Pioneers. They're looking at her with great curiosity. She feels like an animal in a zoo. "I'm on my way to lunch; what's going on?"

The boy closest to Gerhard is tall and gawky. His uniform shirt is partly untucked. "You were right, Gerhard," he says, without taking his eyes off her. "She does look pretty normal. You'd never know."

"I told you," Gerhard says, his voice as even and calm as always.

"Okay, well, I'm off," Marta says, not really caring about whatever weird thing the Young Pioneers are up to.

"They don't serve Coca-Cola in our cafeteria," the tall boy says. "Or American food."

"I know that." She turns to Gerhard. "What's your problem? Get out of the way."

"My friends were wondering if you could tell a traitor just by looking at them. I said I knew the sister of one, if they wanted to see for themselves."

Marta shoves him. Hard. He goes reeling backward. His heel catches on the shoe of the Pioneer behind him and he goes down, flailing his arms.

"Fight!" someone calls from down the corridor. Students begin to crowd around. Marta's vision flickers like an old light bulb. Voices race through her mind. The other Pioneers help Gerhard up. The tall boy gets in her face. Flecks of spittle dot the air in front of his open mouth. The world slows down. For a moment, it's actually pleasant. Like being cushioned in something pure while her stress floats away.

A hand lands heavy on her shoulder. Fingers dig in. The world snaps back into place.

The hand spins her around. Frau Vandenburg scowls at her. She looks furious.

"Come with me right now!" she commands. Without loosening her grip on Marta's shoulder, she marches her back inside the classroom and shoves her down into a chair. Then she slams the classroom door. She folds her arms and peers down at Marta with unblinking eyes that fill the lenses of her glasses. Marta feels like she's being examined by an enormous doll. Her heart is racing. Swirling visions fly through her mind—pummeling Gerhard till his face bleeds, his dumb friends prying her off, kicking and screaming and scratching . . .

"What are we going to do with you?" Frau Vandenburg asks.

"Let me go to lunch?" Marta says without thinking.

Frau Vandenburg's face does many things at once. She turns the color of a star on a Soviet tank. Marta braces herself for an explosion of fury. Instead, to Marta's surprise, Frau Vandenburg closes her eyes and takes a series of deep breaths. When she opens her eyes, she calmly places a chair across the desk from Marta, sits down, and folds her hands.

"Your mother was a teacher in the West, was she not?"

Marta hesitates. "Yes. Before the wall went up."

"The Anti-Fascist Protection Barrier," Frau Vandenburg corrects her gently.

Everybody just calls it the wall, she thinks. "Yes, Frau Vandenburg."

"And what does she do now?"

An alarm bell rings in Marta's head. Shouldn't she be in big trouble? Shouldn't Frau Vandenburg be yelling at her for shoving Gerhard? This little conversation is more troubling than being screamed at or punished with detention.

"She works in a washing machine factory."

"Because our labor exchange reassigned her."

"Yes."

Marta finds that her heart is still pounding. Her hands tremble. She makes a fist underneath the desk, grinds her knuckles into her thigh.

Frau Vandenburg's whole demeanor is gentle. "How does she feel about this?"

Marta treads carefully. "She liked being a teacher. This job got chosen for her, so she's not as happy doing it."

"Ah. Happiness," Frau Vandenburg says as if she's just solved a mystery. "There we have it." She smiles, triumphant. "This is further proof that the protection barrier is one hundred percent necessary. To put it simply, Marta, your mother has been poisoned by the West—by this idea that working purely for your own satisfaction will bring you happiness. I would venture to say your entire family has been poisoned in this way. Your brother was—"

"Don't talk about my brother!" she blurts out. She feels reckless, out of control, balanced on a razor's edge. Everybody wants to use Stefan as some kind of symbol. Nobody cares that he was just a nice kid who liked swimming and Digedags and eating frites with way too much mayonnaise.

THWACK. Frau Vandenburg slaps her palm down on the desk. "Don't you raise your voice at me, Marta Dietrich. Who do you think you are?"

Marta doesn't say a word.

"I'll tell you who you are," Frau Vandenburg says. "You are no more or less special than any of us. You are in my class so that I can prepare you to become a worker advancing the cause of international socialism. That is your purpose." She swivels and points at the board. "Right now, there are eight countries in the Warsaw Pact. Perhaps you will live long enough to see dozens more, as our revolution spreads across the globe." She turns back to Marta. "I envy your youth. I don't want to see you squander it on the empty promises of the West. To that end, I believe you need more strict education than I can provide. Starting next week, you will be joining Gerhard in the Young Pioneers. Perhaps then you will learn the proper respect for our movement."

Marta opens her mouth to protest.

"And," Frau Vandenburg cuts in, "you will have an extra homework assignment. You will watch *The Black Channel* every week and write a report about Herr von Schnitzler's thoughts on immoral Western TV programs. Now, go eat your lunch."

Frau Vandenburg gets up and replaces the chair behind the neighboring desk. Then she leaves the room. Cafeteria sounds drift in through the open door. Marta imagines she can hear Gerhard and the Young Pioneers among them, laughing at how they provoked the traitor's sister.

She closes her eyes. Her future—the future Frau Vandenburg just planned out for her—stretches into the darkness. A red necktie and a white collared shirt. *A worker advancing the cause.* Assigned, like her mother, to a job she doesn't get to choose. A cog in the vast machine that executed her brother without a second thought, then branded him a traitor.

More countries in the Warsaw Pact.

More lines on the chalkboard.

She opens her eyes and goes to the front of the class, where she picks up an eraser and swipes it across the eight nations, back and forth, until the chalkboard is empty.

Marta Dietrich has made up her mind.

You did *what*?"

Alma Dietrich's hands go to her face, covering her mouth and forming a little steeple to frame her nose. Marta has never seen her mother perform such a theatrical gesture before. She looks like an actress in one of the DEFA musical comedy films. Except there's nothing funny about the three of them shivering on the roof of their apartment block while heavy snow blankets Berlin.

Or maybe there is. Marta is having a hard time distinguishing funny from sad, ridiculous from dangerous. She still feels like she hasn't slept in days.

"I went to see Harry at the kneipe yesterday after school," she says. "He told me the escape plan's divided up into compartments, in case anybody gets caught and tortured. He couldn't tell you about it because the Stasi are keeping such a close eye on us. See, it was my job to make the Stasi *think* the plan was to take a DR train from Dresden, even though that isn't true. Harry called it *misdirection*. At first I was mad about all this stuff, but I think it actually makes a lot of sense."

Her mother lowers her hands and curses out loud. "I should have let you wring that idiot's neck, Pieter."

"You talked to Harry at the kneipe," her father says in disbelief. The collar of his overcoat is flipped up. Fresh snow glistens in his unruly hair.

"Well, in the alley outside," Marta explains. "They didn't really want me to come in."

"Ah," her father says. "The alley outside the kneipe. Much better."

They are huddled together in the center of the roof, near the fire door, so they can't be seen from the street below. Marta follows her father's eyes as they drift across the border fence to cousin Markus's building. The dragon's teeth wear cloaks of white. The snow is falling so heavily she can barely pick out her cousin's window.

"I wonder what Markus is doing right now," she says.

Her father fixes her with a pained expression. "I'm worried that you think life is so much better in the West. That it's some kind of paradise. But there are rules there too, you know."

"And anyway," her mother says sharply, "you're twelve years old. You'd be doing what other people want no matter which side of the city we're living in."

"What about when I grow up?" Marta says. "What if I want to be a teacher and they force me to work in a washing machine factory?"

"We make the best of what we are given," her mother insists. "We do what we have to do, and we love each other as best we can, no matter where we are. Our lives aren't defined by our work."

"That's not what Frau Vandenburg says. She says I'm to be a worker advancing the cause of the socialist revolution around the world. That's my purpose."

Now it's her father's turn to curse. "I wish I could wring *her* neck."

"Pieter!" her mother says. "That's enough talk of neck-wringing for one evening."

"You started it," he points out.

"That's true." She turns to Marta. "Violence is never the answer."

"I shoved Gerhard in the hall today."

Her parents look at each other.

"Marta," her mother says, "I appreciate that you're honoring our promise to stop keeping secrets from each other. But my shift starts in an hour and I can't be late again."

"Yes," her father says. "How many more secrets could you possibly have?" He pauses to stick out his tongue and let a few snowflakes settle on it. Then he runs a hand through his hair and wipes it on the front of his coat. "And why have you dragged us up to the roof in the middle of a snowstorm?"

"I needed to talk to you up here in case our apartment is bugged," Marta explains. "So here goes. Harry's leaving tonight, on a U-Bahn train." She lets that sink in for a moment. "All we have to do is be on the platform at the Bernauer Strasse station in the first minute of Christmas Eve. 12:01. And he'll pick us up."

Her father laughs oddly, in a way that says to Marta: *This is the least funny thing I have ever heard.*

"Will he now! Our chauffeur to the West. I don't know whether Harry is working for the Stasi, or whether he means well and is just a fool, but the tra-pos closed the Bernauer Strasse station as soon as the wall went up, back in August."

"I know," Marta says. She thinks back to the first conversation she overheard between Helmut and Harry, poised outside the door to the air shaft. *Ghost stations.* "We just have to find a way to get down there, and—"

"You're not listening!" her mother says. "Harry might be a fool and a dreamer, but he's right about the Stasi paying us too much attention right now. Which is why we can't do anything rash. If—and this is a big if—there comes a time one day when we decide *as a family*, after careful consideration, to cross over to the West, then there are safer ways of doing so."

"The candy-cane man said they're going to put you in prison at Hohenschönhausen unless I become an informer and tell on Harry!" she blurts out. "That's why we have to leave! It's like we're caught in a great big web that we're never going to get out of if we stay here."

Her father raises his eyes to the falling snow. "The candy-cane man."

"His name is Lothar," Marta says. She doesn't bother to add *he's Stasi*. It's obvious.

"Hohenschönhausen," her mother says. She turns her back and paces across the roof to the edge overlooking the courtyard. The name of the prison makes Marta's skin crawl. She recalls Lothar's jolly talk of "treatments" in cells where the lights never come on.

"I'm sorry, Papa," Marta says.

"It's all right," he says. He sounds stunned. "It's not your fault. After what happened with Stefan, they were bound to find some reason to send us there sooner or later. I just thought it would be more toward the *later* side of things. I thought we'd all have more time together, before . . ." He trails off. "Before it all fell apart."

Her mother comes back to them. "We're leaving tonight," she announces.

"Alma," Marta's father says, "there are other ways. I know people at the Ministry who might be able to help."

"Who, Gabrielle? She cleans the floors." Her mother gives them both the Teacher Look. "No. I can't believe I'm saying this, but Marta's right. We *are* caught in a web, and it's only going to get worse. There's no more time to wait to see how things play out. We cannot use that as an excuse to do nothing. To remain stuck here." She pulls Marta in close. "The other night, at the kitchen table. You were right about that too. They killed your brother, and they lied about him in the papers. This country doesn't *deserve* to have you grow up inside its walls, Marta."

Her father looks out across the rooftops. Marta can't see very far in any direction. The spire of the Zionskirche is a ghostly spike piercing the storm. The border fence is lost in a haze, weaving in and out of sight as the snow blows nearly sideways. "If this keeps up," he says quietly, "the snow will bury the wall. And we'll be one city again."

"Until it melts," Marta says.

Her father looks at her. "Yes," he says, "that's right. Until it melts." He takes them both by their hands. His fingers are ice cold and his grip is firm. "Let's do this, then."

"For Stefan," Marta says.

"For all of us," her mother says.

Thirty minutes to midnight.

The Bernauer Strasse station once boasted a proud sign, a giant U for U-Bahn that marked the entrance. Now there is only a sad, snow-covered lump rising from the pavement: an army-green tarpaulin stretched across the top of the staircase. The trapos have done their best to erase it from the map of East Berlin.

When they first left the apartment, Marta thought the snow was a blessing. It has been coming down for hours with no sign of letting up, a cosmic stroke of luck sent to conceal them. It's beautiful, wet, packing snow, the kind Stefan used to make perfect little snowballs, which he called "artillery." Her boots squelch as they sink down into it.

But now that they're approaching the station, she's twitchy and anxious. There's nobody else out. Anyone with any sense is huddled inside under blankets, with steaming cups of tea. The snow isn't camouflage; it's a backdrop that makes them stand out. Three dark figures leaning into the wind, a trio on a strange and suspicious errand.

Falling snow fills the cones of light cast down from streetlamps. The air smells fresh and cool, like a mountain stream has been flash frozen and dumped on the city. Fear is a cold fist in her belly.

Marta hugs Penelope to her chest. The warm little puppy is swaddled in the carrier that Marta's mother used for her and Stefan when they were infants. Penelope whimpers softly.

"It's okay," Marta whispers. "I know this is weird. Soon we'll be inside again." She reaches into her pocket and feeds Penelope a dried beef treat. The puppy's tongue warms her fingers.

Besides Penelope, she carries nothing. Even if there had been more time to pack, they can't risk being stopped by a grepo on patrol. How would it look to be carrying luggage down the street in the middle of the night? They might as well hold signs that say We Are Crossing the Border.

At least with Penelope, they can say they're taking her to the vet for an emergency. *She ate a whole onion, sir!* A feeble story, perhaps, but at least it's something.

Her father carries a pair of bolt cutters in the large pocket of his overcoat. If a grepo approaches, he'll have to drop them in the snow.

Her mother carries a single photograph of Stefan on the banks of the Orankesee, digging his toes into the sand.

Marta thinks of their abandoned apartment. The Riga clock ticking away on the wall. The lines on the chalkboard. The Digedags comics spread out on the coffee table. A museum of their lives here in the East.

They reach the mound marking the entrance to the station. It rises from a little concrete island at the point where Bernauer Strasse meets Brunnenstrasse. A row of snow-covered Trabants form a long bumpy spine, like a sea monster's bones. Somewhere, a dog barks, and Penelope wriggles in her carrier. Marta feeds her another beef treat.

"Big night for you," she whispers. Her father reaches down into the snow and fumbles for the edge of the tarp. Marta looks up at the apartment blocks that line the street, silent and mostly dark. Here and there a light burns. How many eyes are on them now? She glances over her shoulder. Their footprints have left a trail in the deep snow, easy for anyone to follow.

"I think it's pinned down somehow," her father says, "like a tent."

"Cut it," her mother says, head on a swivel. "Hurry."

He kneels down in a deep snowdrift that seems to swallow him up to the waist. Marta hears a smooth *shnick* as he runs the blade of the cutting tool in a line from the ground, up through the plastic covering.

She takes one last look at the street where she's lived her entire life. Whatever happens—whether they make it out, or the trapos shoot them down, or the Stasi arrest them—they won't be coming back. She pictures the empty apartment one last time, then banishes it from her mind.

A moment later, they're ducking inside the newly made flap. Marta imagines a grepo walking by and seeing the tarp moving around like a costume for a play with three hapless actors flailing about inside. It's dark and smelly under the tarp. Damp, sour air drifts up from the platform below, along with murky subterranean noises—distant U-Bahn trains rushing past other ghost stations on the line. She hugs Penelope tight.

A metal grate beneath their feet covers what used to be the top of the stairs—the entrance to the station. Her father presses the teeth of the bolt cutter against one of the grate's bars, no thicker than chain link. He's beginning to squeeze the handles when voices come up from below. Two men in conversation. One of them laughs. It's impossible to tell how far away they are—at the bottom of the staircase or out across the platform.

Trapos, Marta thinks. Her heart is hammering. Penelope squirms against her.

Her father mutters a low curse. There is no choice but to keep going—if they miss this chance, there won't be another like it. And the only thing waiting for them if they remain in the East is Hohenschönhausen prison. In the dim light, Marta watches her father tense his body to cut the metal as carefully as he can. She holds her breath.

The link snaps in half with a *click*. It's not loud, but it's not exactly silent either. She listens: There's no sudden change in the banter of the trapos down below. Her father exhales. He moves to the next link, and the next, and the next, squeezing the bolt cutters with a methodical rhythm. Marta zones out, focusing on listening to the trapos. She can pick out the odd word. They are talking about who did what last night at the beer hall.

Gossip: the pastime of everyone in East Berlin (and maybe the entire world, for all Marta knows). Whether you're in secondary school or the border police or the Stasi, it's all about who said what to whom.

She has no time to reflect on the oddness of this. Her father is almost done with his careful snipping. Together with her mother, they bend to the grate and work their hands through gaps in the metal. Penelope settles hard against Marta's chest.

"Last one," her father whispers. "Hold tight."

Marta grips as hard as she can. A horrific vision flashes in her mind: the metal grate falling, clattering down the stairs, alerting the trapos below and the grepos patrolling the length of the wall.

Snip.

The last link gives way. The grate does not fall. Her father pockets the bolt cutters, and together the Dietrichs lift the large metal square and move it carefully aside. Maneuvering a heavy grate on their knees underneath a tarp should be really hard to do, but Marta finds that she can lift it with little effort, that her muscles aren't straining at all. She suspects it has something to do with her pounding heart and the blood rushing in her ears. *Adrenaline.*

The power of pure fear.

With the square cutout set on the grate next to it, there's now a hole the size of her bedroom window. Stepping lightly on tiptoes, she descends. The only light is a blue-tinted glow coming from the platform. It feels like they're heading toward an indoor pool in the basement of an empty schwimmhalle. The kind of place Stefan and her father would go to practice starting off the blocks, for hours and hours.

At the bottom of the stairs, the passage fans out into the wide mezzanine that Marta thinks of as the "old station," built in the early days of the U-Bahn. There are beautiful glass booths with narrow windowpanes and iron benches bolted to the concrete floor. Marta and her parents creep behind one of the booths, which used to be a news vendor. Copies of *Neues Deutschland* and *Sibylle* plaster the sides of the booth, all of them from August 12—the last day before the wall went up and the station shut down for good. The damp smell is potent down here. Melted snow drips down through girders and pools in shimmery patches on the concrete.

From their hiding place, they can peer above the old papers and magazines, through the glass, and out to the platform. A pair of floodlights with skinny posts for bodies and big lamps for heads has been set up near the pillars that line the platform. At the edge closest to the tracks are two trapos smartly dressed in their uniforms and caps.

The men peer down into the darkness of the tunnel.

A soft beam of light plays along the tiled wall opposite the platform. It sweeps along the black sign that says BERNAUER STRASSE, getting brighter. Marta watches, feeling uneasy, as a dark figure emerges from the tunnel.

The sound of whistling carries across the platform. Marta tenses. She clutches Penelope tightly and pets the top of her head.

Marta's father holds out his wrist so she and her mother can see the face of his watch.

Five minutes to midnight.

The two young trapos lean out over the tracks and reach down to help the third man up to the platform. His torch sends the beam of light spinning crazily across the tiled walls as he's lifted up. Then he clicks it off, brushes soot from the front of his overcoat, and claps one of the men chummily on the back.

"A fine night to catch some border jumpers red-handed, don't you think?"

Marta's heart pounds. The man is without his shaggy hair and his American beatnik attitude. There's no candy cane in sight. Yet she recognizes the voice: Lothar the Stasi agent.

"Yes, sir!" the trapos reply in unison.

"I checked the barricade, where the track splits west. It's quite intact." Marta feels her parents tense up. Barricade? Does Harry know about this? "We should be in for quite a show if they make a run for it. So!" He rubs his gloved hands together. "Who's got coffee?"

She can sense nervousness on the part of the trapos. They look at each other, then one of them clears his throat. "Sir, we were wondering—where is the rest of your team? Why is it only you here?"

"Where's the full weight of the Stasi, you mean?" Lothar grins. "You won't believe this, but my assistant and the rest of my people have been dispatched to Dresden. You see, we picked up some advance intelligence that this escape would be originating from there, using a DR steam train. I'd be there too, right now, scratching my head in the cold, if it weren't for a last-minute tip from a highly placed informer."

Marta feels a strange combination of excitement that her misdirection job actually worked and horror that they were betrayed by an informer.

She thinks of the strange faces leering at her from the tables in the kneipe.

Frau Vandenburg.

Herr Schmidt.

Anyone and everyone. Lies and suspicion. The foundation of East Berlin.

Lothar folds his arms, smiling at the trapos, who have fallen silent. The reality of discussing informers with a Stasi agent is uncomfortable, even for trapos. Plenty of guards have abandoned their posts and crossed the border themselves, after all. One of those former guards is a tally mark on her father's chalkboard.

"You can always count on the Young Pioneers to keep a vigilant eye out," Lothar says.

Marta closes her eyes. *Gerhard.* Of course. She's not even surprised. She should have known.

"What time do you have?" Lothar says.

Marta opens her eyes. One of the trapos glances at his wrist. "One minute to midnight."

Lothar steps to the edge of the platform and glances up the tracks. "I see the lights. It won't be long now." He draws a pistol from inside his coat. "Happy Christmas, gentlemen. Let's all enjoy the gift we're about to receive."

Marta despairs. How are they supposed to cross the platform, past an armed Stasi agent and two trapos, to get to the train? Harry didn't give her any instructions. She had imagined the train pulling up to the platform and opening its doors, as if it were making a normal stop to let commuters on and off. She realizes now how silly that is.

Penelope seems to agree. She squirms against Marta's chest. Then her little paws scrabble against Marta's collarbone. Something has spooked her. Marta whispers, *"Shhhh, it's okay,"* in the puppy's ear. But Penelope keeps on scrambling like she wants to climb out of her carrier and run back upstairs to the snowy street, to the apartment, home. Marta can't blame her.

Her father displays his watch. Midnight.

Penelope lets out a shrill yelp—the kind she uses when she's hungry or needs to go out.

Lothar and the trapos turn to look toward the entrance to the station.

The two trapos draw their own pistols.

Marta tries to clamp a hand around the puppy's snout to keep her mouth shut, but Penelope is quicker. She gets her little teeth around the side of Marta's fingers to prop her mouth open.

Then Penelope wriggles and writhes and lets out a series of loud barks that echo around the station, bouncing off the pillars and the iron beams and the tiles across the tracks.

Lothar aims his pistol at the news vendor's booth.

The station rumbles as the train approaches.

"Penelope, I presume!" the Stasi man calls out with good cheer. "You can all come out now. It's over."

"Stay down!" Marta's father says, gripping her arm.

With his other hand he takes the bolt cutters from his coat pocket. Marta wonders what on earth he's going to do with them. He vibrates with a strange energy.

Foul air, stirred by the oncoming train, rushes through the station. One of the trapos loses his cap. It bounces away down the platform. Lothar heads straight for their hiding place, aiming his weapon. His good cheer has vanished. His mouth is set in a grim line.

Penelope barks and barks.

The train roars into the station in a blur of mustard yellow, too fast to make out the figure in the conductor's compartment. Behind the glass booth, Marta watches in despair—it's going to speed right past and leave them here for good!

Then several things happen at once.

The banshee shriek of a speeding U-Bahn train hitting its brakes, the blast of a pistol shot, and the hollow *thwack* of the bullet ricocheting off cement. Marta sees the trapos run for cover behind pillars. She doesn't think one of them fired, and she knows the Stasi man didn't—he's still coming toward their hiding place, moving relentlessly, undeterred by what's happening around him. His eyes meet Marta's through the glass. He shouts something at her—a single word—but it's lost in the pained howl of the rapidly slowing train.

"We have to run for it!" her mother says in her ear. But Lothar is *right there*, positioned between their hiding place and the train. The hand that grips his pistol is perfectly steady.

The shriek dies away. The train slows to a crawl but doesn't come to a full stop. Marta can read the number on the side of one of its cars, painted in black: 874. A hand extends out one of the train's open windows, holding a silver pistol. The weapon jerks up, the shot rings out, and a second bullet ricochets off one of the pillars, keeping the trapos pinned down. A single eye behind the train window glints in the blue light of the platform. Helmut.

A third shot sends a chunk of concrete spinning inches from Lothar's heels. The Stasi man dives out of the way, hits the ground, and comes up smoothly on one knee to fire his weapon back at the train.

Helmut vanishes from the window. Lothar's shots ping into the train's yellow siding. A constellation of silver pocks the metal.

The final train car glides past, empty tracks in its wake. This is their last chance. Harry's wife, Monika, stands in a half-open door, beckoning, her eyes wide with fear. Helmut reappears in the window and resumes firing. One of the trapos leans out from beside the pillar and lets off a wild shot of his own. A chunk of ceiling crashes down. Acrid smoke begins to gather on the platform.

Penelope has gone silent.

"Now!" Marta's father says. Marta emerges from behind the newspaper booth. She doesn't even try to stay low, or zigzag, or do anything but sprint headlong across the platform to the train as it crosses the halfway point.

It is now officially leaving the station. Leaving them behind.

"Faster!" Monika screams.

But to get to the train, they have to run right past Lothar. He straightens up to block their way.

Marta can see the black hole in the barrel of his pistol widen to the size of her thumb as she gets closer.

His mouth moves. He is oddly calm. "No one has to die," he says.

Suddenly, her father moves past her with the quicksilver grace of a swimmer leaping off the blocks into the water. His arm comes up and down in a split second. There's a flash of cold steel. The heavy bolt cutters slam into Lothar's forearm. His face contorts in shock and pain. The pistol goes flying from his grip.

Her father whirls halfway around, grabs her arm, and propels her forward. Her legs burn as she keeps pace with the train. It slows a tiny bit to allow them to catch up. Monika wrenches the door wide open. Marta feels her feet leave the ground as her father *flings* her into the waiting car. The world blurs. The platform disappears. A soft, strong hand takes hold of her and eases her in for a landing. The floor of the train feels solid yet springy with the energy coursing through the tracks beneath her feet. Faces appear— Monika, who's slowing her down, embracing her, depositing her into a seat, all at the same time. Hans, Joachim, Ingrid, even Gerhard, looking both glum and furious. She pets Penelope. Her hands shake. She glances around wildly. There is her mother. And her father. Both of them cling to a vertical pole.

The train doors begin to close. Marta exhales—but her breath catches in her throat when the doors close on a gloved hand. The hand works its way in and becomes an arm, then a torso. Lothar begins to wriggle inside.

"Harry!" Monika screams at the front of the car. "Faster!"

Marta's mother reaches out and grabs Lothar's arm. She bends his elbow and tries to shove him out. Her father braces himself against the pole and tries to slide the door shut with both hands, but Lothar still manages to widen the gap. More than half his body is inside the car. Marta rushes from her seat, seizes his leg, and lifts up with all her strength. Lothar cries out. She keeps on lifting. Her father sees what she's doing and abandons the door to grab on to the leg with both hands.

Lothar begins to fall back.

Together, Marta and her father twist the Stasi agent's leg while her mother shoves his body as hard as she can. He falls out of the train.

Still, the doors won't shut all the way. Lothar's ankle is trapped. Marta and her father twist so that his toes are pointing downward. Lothar cries out. They push until his foot pops out and the doors slam shut, just as the last car leaves the platform behind and heads into the tunnel.

Out the back window, Marta watches the trapos rush out from behind the pillar to the Stasi man's aid. He is rolling back and forth on the floor of the platform, clutching his leg. Then the train picks up speed and clatters around a bend and the platform vanishes. There is only the dark tunnel behind them now.

The speakers in the train car crackle. Harry's garbled voice, barely audible, comes over the intercom. "Hold on! We're switching tracks."

Marta and her parents squish together on one of the benches. Harry's announcement reminds her of what the Stasi man said about the barricade. "Wait!"

Monika meets her eyes.

"They blocked off the tracks!"

"There's no way to call up to Harry!" she says. "The intercom is one way!"

"He'll be expecting it," her father says. "Don't worry."

He sounds very worried.

There's a sudden jolt. Marta clutches her father's arm. Penelope yelps. A few more bumps, and the train seems to click into place. Marta's eyes roam the train car. Gerhard looks down at his feet. He's not wearing his Young Pioneers uniform. Marta wonders if they had to drag him onto the train kicking and screaming. She can't believe he would actually rat out his own father's escape plan.

This entire family should probably have a long talk when they get to the West.

"We're speeding up," her mother says.

Marta feels a rush in the pit of her stomach that says: This train is practically airborne. Outside the windows, the tunnel is pitch-black. It's as if they're hurtling through a void.

"We're going to crash through!" Harry shouts into the intercom. He makes a noise like a war cry. Then the intercom goes silent.

Marta closes her eyes and thinks of her brother and his crossing. The darkness of the tunnel and the darkness of the harbor. She can feel him beside her. Beside them all.

When they hit the barrier, the energy of the collision thunders through the train cars. A buckling, grinding sensation courses through the floor and up her legs to settle in the pit of her stomach. Her mother's elbow comes up and smashes her in the side of the face. She opens her eyes. The noise of the crash seems to come from an expanding storm in the very center of her skull. A bottle skitters across the floor.

The train tilts and scrapes the side of the tunnel wall. This time there is a shower of sparks to accompany the shriek. Lights flicker, die, and come back up. The train tilts back on an even keel. Debris flies past the windows, skims the walls, rattles against the train, and shoots out into their wake. Marta watches pieces of the barrier bounce away up the tracks.

The train slows down. The noise in her head dies away. She looks around at the faces of her family. Astonishment, fear, wild-eyed madness. The little kids are crying. Gerhard looks stunned. Monika is up and about, attending to them all, heedless of the motion.

The intercom crackles. Harry's voice fills the car.

"Attention, Dietrichs! Allow me to be the first to welcome you to West Berlin."

Stasi Headquarters
The House of a Thousand Eyes

On Lothar Muller's first day back at work following his release from the hospital, they bake him a *kuchen*. It's waiting for him in the lunchroom near his office. Two layers of chocolate filled with cream and cherries soaked in schnapps. Klaus, along with a dozen of his closest colleagues, are standing at the small round table. Everyone applauds when he enters the room. The clapping stabs little bursts of pain into his head, just behind his eyes. He takes a moment to force a smile and orders himself to stay put. It takes all his willpower not to back out of the room and head for the solitude of his office. One thing that keeps him here is this: It is difficult for him to back up and reverse course on crutches. He's still getting used to moving forward.

He does so now, planting the crutches, feeling the pressure in his armpits as he lifts his wounded leg. It feels awkward to move this way in front of men and women he's guided, commanded, and counseled. Subordinates who view him with that vital mixture of respect and fear. He scans their eyes, the windows to their grubby little scheming souls. He sees the gears turning in their minds, weighing new truths, new judgments about the man they serve.

A man who failed to prevent the biggest mass escape yet. Nine people. Nine! And if it weren't for that ten-year-old boy, an informer in the Young Pioneers, he wouldn't have gotten as close as he did. He would have been in Dresden, with Klaus and the rest of them, preparing to stop a Christmas Day escape that never came.

He thinks of the chalkboard in the kitchen of Alma, Pieter, and Marta Dietrich's flat. The eleven tally marks, one for each border crosser killed in the attempt.

Now, the nine who escaped practically cancel them out.

He manages to put together a few words of thanks. He endures another round of applause, this one more tepid, which begins and ends quickly.

Klaus sinks a huge knife into the cake. Another colleague takes a small plate from a stack on the table. Everyone laughs politely at the size of the slice—*you won't have to eat again for days, Lothar!* He accepts the plate hesitantly, balanced on his crutches. He refuses to let them see him sink into a chair, even though his aching body is screaming to sit down.

His leg throbs. There's a sort of fiery numbness that comes and goes in his dangling left foot. He smiles obligingly at his colleagues' jokes and watches them as they eat. The kuchen tastes like dirt. Dizziness takes hold and he sets his plate down on the table before he drops it. All around him, jaws move and teeth chew up coconut frosting and cherries and chocolate. Crumbs get stuck in the corners of mouths and cascade down ugly neckties. He feels sick. He wants to crawl back into his hospital bed and close his eyes to ride the calming waves of the morphine drip.

After a while, he makes an excuse, something about catching up with the pile of work that's waiting for him on his desk. Everyone seems relieved. He notes how quickly they rush to clean their plates and go back to their own responsibilities.

As he plants his rubber-tipped crutches on the linoleum and swings his wounded leg in the direction of his office, he analyzes the mood from the little party. The subtle differences in the way his team acted around him. It's like they're already beginning to distance themselves, as if being too close to such a spectacular failure could be damaging to their careers.

Guilty by association.

He has to smile grimly at that as he reaches the door to his office. How many East Berliners are at this very moment languishing in a prison cell because the Stasi deemed them guilty by association?

He can't get his door open fast enough. He finds that he's beginning to sweat from the exertion of moving himself down the corridor. His underarms feel bruised.

Inside, he shuts the door behind him and grits his teeth against another burning stab inside his leg. The smell of his office is familiar, yet strange and a little depressing, like bumping into an old school friend who pretends not to know who you are. (Which happens often when you work for the Stasi.) He makes his way over to his desk, props his crutches against the wall, and lowers himself into his worn-out chair.

It turns out that the pile of work wasn't just a convenient excuse. The secretaries have loaded his desk with towers of paper, walls of documents, battlements of file folders. A fortress of paperwork. He slides the mountain of documents and their carbon copies aside.

His breath catches in his throat.

A ghastly face stares up from his desk. White as a blank sheet of paper.

It takes him a moment to recognize Lenin's death mask, cast in plaster. Just like the one in the Supervisor's office. Next to it is a small card, like the one he slipped to the girl, Marta. On it is written *Welcome Back.—Mielke.*

A gift from the Supervisor himself. Three weeks ago, before his great failure, Muller would have been proud to receive such a thing. Now, the legendary communist stares up at him with disgust. And what to make of the note from the Supervisor? "Welcome Back"?

He analyzes it from every angle. Perhaps, if he were in a different line of work—a factory worker or a delivery man—such a note could be taken at face value. The big boss welcoming back a valued and injured employee. Simple. But that's not how things work at the highest level of the House of a Thousand Eyes.

Two words, infinite meanings.

Muller is very tired. He stares at the photo of Ulbricht on the wall and lets his eyes go out of focus.

A sharp knock at the door shakes him from his reverie.

"Come in!" he calls, sitting up in his chair, busily shuffling papers.

His assistant, Klaus, enters and shuts the door softly behind him. Then he stands stiffly at attention.

Muller regards him curiously for a moment. *What am I supposed to do?*

Ah yes. He waves his hand toward the empty chair on the other side of his desk. "Come in. Have a seat."

"Thank you, sir." Klaus sits down. His eyes catch Lenin's plaster face on the desk and he looks up, puzzled.

"A gift," Muller says, "from Supervisor Mielke." He can't shake the weary resignation in his voice.

"That's very kind of him," Klaus says.

"Yes, Erich Mielke is renowned throughout Germany for his legendary kindness," Muller says. He is astonished, even as he speaks, at the bitterness in his voice. *Stupid, Lothar. Rein it in. Control yourself.*

Klaus frowns. He shifts in his seat, flustered, unsure of what to say. *This is how they will treat me now,* Muller thinks. *All of them. Like failure is contagious and I am infecting them with mine.*

"Did you enjoy your party?" Klaus asks brightly.

"Yes," Muller says. "What a wonderful surprise. Thank you."

"We all chipped in for the cake," he says.

"It was delicious. My favorite."

There is a long silence. Muller can't find the words to fill it. He knows what he should be saying to his subordinate. Confident words. Angry words. Great motivating speeches about working twice as hard so this never happens again. Dedicating their lives to making sure every last traitor is locked up or dead. This kind of thing used to come so easily to him. Now it's like the pain in his leg reaches all the way up into his mind, strangling his thoughts. Turning them inward.

Klaus scratches his knee. Muller notes the "tell"—the giveaway that something serious is on his mind. Ordinarily, he would warn Klaus to eliminate all his tells. Be a blank canvas to project different identities upon. His eyes flick to his wigs and the other odds and ends of his disguises. For the first time ever, they strike him as silly. A child's game.

"I wanted to apologize," Klaus says at last.

"For what?"

"Before the operation, we spoke in your office. I know I was hesitant to act. I displayed sympathy for this girl, Marta Dietrich, because of what happened to her brother back in November. The traitor who attempted to swim Humboldt Harbor."

"I recall."

"I wanted you to know that I'm prepared to do everything possible to see that these people are brought to justice. After what happened to you, we can't afford to be lenient. We have to send a message."

Muller is taken aback. "Brought to justice? My boy, I'm not sure if you noticed, but the Dietrichs have already crossed over to the West. The opportunity for justice has come and gone."

Klaus lowers his voice. "There is always Unit 46."

Muller is taken aback. The very existence of the Stasi kidnapping squad is top secret, even to most Stasi agents. Klaus has been doing some digging. "There is no such thing," he says.

Klaus smiles thinly. "Of course not. But if there was such a unit, who could track down traitors in the West and have them brought back across the border to pay for their crimes—to pay for what they did to you—then I would be honored to assist them."

Muller places his hands upon the mountain of papers in front of him and peers over the top at his assistant. A stab of pain stirs up fragments of memory.

Falling backward out of the train car as it picks up speed.

The doors slamming shut on his ankle.

The feel of the cement scraping his back as he's dragged along.

The look on the girl's face as she twists his leg with all her might.

He has caught border crossers in the act before, down in the tunnels and the sewers, but he has never looked into their eyes.

What he saw in Marta's haunts him. A desperate, animal defiance.

"That won't be necessary," Muller says.

"Sir?"

"We will leave them be."

Klaus hesitates. "With all due respect, sir—people all over the Ministry are talking. They're saying it's the biggest escape we've ever had. I was just thinking it might be best to pursue them immediately."

"To save face."

"Yes. For your career, I mean."

"And yours, you mean."

"I only want what's best for our country."

Muller shuffles a document pointlessly from one pile to another. "What would be best for our country is if we tore down that wall."

Klaus's eyes widen. He glances at the door, leans forward, and lowers his voice to a whisper. "Perhaps you came back to work too soon, sir. Perhaps you should go home and rest some more."

"Do you remember when you told me about your dream of a monstrous wall cutting all of Europe in half?"

"Yes."

"And do you remember what I told you? That people will get used to anything over time?"

"I do."

Marta's face is etched in his mind. Fearful, yes. But also determined beyond belief. Willing to risk everything for a chance at a new life in the

West. "I was wrong about that." How many more Marta Dietrichs are there out there, biding their time, planning their escapes? "I don't believe they will ever accept this wall."

"But for every Marta there are five Gerhards. We will have no shortage of information on these traitors."

"Ah," Muller says, "Gerhard. Our Young Pioneer boy. You know, we have been studying our informers for years to try to find out why they do it. What's in it for them? After all, we don't pay these people."

"Sir, I must insist that you take some more time to get yourself together."

"Do you know what we've come to find out? Informing on their friends and family is *its own reward*. They simply like having a bit of an advantage over other people, even if it never amounts to very much. That's all. It makes them feel like they're *somebody*." He laughs. Klaus squirms in his chair, looking like he'd rather be anywhere else. "What does that say about us?" Muller's leg throbs. His eyes fill with tears. "No wonder they all want to leave."

JANUARY 27, 1989

The old hotel on the banks of the Dahme River has seen better days. Its crumbling edifice is a portrait of ruin. A patio that once led gracefully down to the edge of the water is home to stray dogs and old iron tables. The once-grand entryway is speckled with pigeon droppings and strewn with garbage. The windows are covered in plywood. A construction scaffold for some long-abandoned restoration project tilts perilously away from an upper floor. Kurt imagines it prying itself free and scampering off on its rusted metal legs.

He stands under a tree across the street and scans the building for signs of recent hauntings. On its own, the hotel might not be so bad, but this whole neighborhood on the eastern fringes of Adlershof seems like the perfect home for restless ghouls. A district of brickyards, warehouses, and empty lots, made no more inviting by the midwinter dusk. Night, falling quickly, drapes the hotel in a curious half darkness that's tricky on the eye.

Kurt uses the rough bark of the trunk to scratch his back. He leans against the tree and watches and waits.

According to the note his grandfather left on the kitchen counter, this is exactly when, and where, Kurt is supposed to contact him. When he thinks back to that evening, he can still hear the *thunk* of his grandfather's cane coming down on the listening devices he so casually revealed. And the man's parting words have been lodged in his head ever since.

You won't win a chess game against the Stasi. We own all the boards, and all the pieces, and we move them whether or not it's our turn.

He curls his fingers and blows hot air into his fists. He shifts his weight from one foot to another. The wind kicks up and the damp chill seems to slither up his sleeves, into his coat, through his skin, into his bones. He wishes Lina were here. But he hasn't even told her about his grandfather's visit. After seeing those bugs, he can't bring himself to talk to anyone about anything.

Now, the darker it gets, the dumber he feels. If the Stasi own all the chessboards and all the pieces, then he is nothing but a pawn at the mercy of a shadowy hand.

Suddenly, a light blinks on and off behind a first-floor window, the only one not boarded up. He rubs his eyes. There it is again—a flashlight, he's sure of it. On-off, on-off, on-off.

Unless there's another secret meeting in the same place at the same time, this must be his cue.

He crosses the street, hands in his pockets, trying to look inconspicuous. He is pretty sure that by overthinking it he's actually moving like a robot.

A stray dog slinks off the front steps and into the shadows. Kurt feels like he's very far from home, even though he's at the edge of the neighborhood he's lived in since he was born. Now that he's decided to go over the wall, every little decision takes him further from the life he knows. He is in uncharted territory. A pawn venturing over the edge of the board.

The hotel doors are long gone. With a pounding heart, he slips into the lobby. He imagines what ghostly hotel guests would look like—ladies in white shrouds holding candles and disappearing down dark hallways . . .

"In here, Kurt."

He spins around, startled. The light flashes from a room behind the wreckage of the front desk. In the gloom he can just barely make out the figure of a man, slightly bent yet still imposing. He makes his way through an archway. A spiderweb sticks to his face. He peels it off.

The room smells of mold. He passes the broken frame of a great hearth. It was cozy in here once, a place for guests to sip drinks by the fire.

"Hi," Kurt says, feeling unbelievably stupid. He should have come up with a better greeting. Something more suitable for a secret meeting in an abandoned hotel.

"So," his grandfather says, "you've made up your mind."

The cane clacks on the filthy floorboards. As he draws closer, he sees the man who emerges from the shadows isn't his grandfather at all. Kurt steps back. This man is much older, with a stringy, unkempt beard, a liver-spotted bald head, and a toothless grin.

"Precautions upon precautions," he says, giving Kurt a moment to get used to the disguise. "Welcome to the finest hotel in Adlershof. Unfortunately, the front desk staff seems to have deserted their post."

Kurt doesn't sense any warmth in his grandfather's words. Lothar has never really felt like a member of his family, and now even less so. "It looks like it used to be nice."

"So it was. We used to host Western diplomats here. Every room was bugged."

Kurt glances around uneasily. The ghosts aren't dead people in this place.

They're echoes of conversations, recorded and kept in some forgotten file in the House of a Thousand Eyes.

"Relax," his grandfather says. "I assure you, there hasn't been a recording device—or a working light switch—in this place for many long years. Which is more than I can say for your apartment. Have you been careful about what you've been saying?"

"I thought you smashed the bugs."

"They've reinstated the surveillance."

"Reinstated?" Kurt says, trying to understand. "They came into the apartment? When?"

"When you and your brother were elsewhere. It isn't difficult. I teach trainees to do it every day. A halfway competent team could have been in and out of your apartment in five minutes."

A chill washes over him that has nothing to do with the winter cold. The notion of Stasi agents creeping around the apartment, opening drawers, prowling through his bedroom. He shivers.

There's a blur of motion. His grandfather's arm comes up. Something soft hits him in the chest. He manages to catch it before it hits the ground.

A backpack.

His grandfather has just flung a backpack at him.

"Open it," he says. Kurt unzips the biggest compartment. He has no idea what to expect. Snakes? A bomb? A spring-loaded camera? He reaches inside.

"Careful," his grandfather says. "Sharp."

Kurt's hand traces a coiled rope. It's made of nylon. Durable and modern, like a mountain climber would use. Deeper in the backpack, his fingers brush smooth metal. His grandfather waits patiently, a light rasp to his measured breathing.

"A grappling hook," Kurt says. The reality of going over the wall hits him all at once. The physical effort required. For some reason he had imagined scrambling up and over the series of barriers like a squirrel. It had been easy enough to gloss over that part of it in his mind. Too much time watching birds out the window of the academy, too little time doing pull-ups on his brother's exercise bar.

"Open the front pouch. Carefully."

Kurt finds a pair of thick slippers with soles covered in rubbery nubs.

"Special shoes," his grandfather says. "For climbing."

"Do you know my size?" he blurts out.

There's a pause. "Forty."

Kurt wonders if he knows that because he's Kurt's grandfather, or because he's a Stasi agent who knows everything about everybody. He can't find the words to ask such a question out loud.

His grandfather clearly thinks he's scared of the prospect of climbing. Which isn't exactly untrue. "I wish there was another way," Lothar says. "But they're watching me. Always."

Kurt is taken aback. "Who is? The Stasi?"

"Of course."

"But you *are* the Stasi." He's heard so many of his grandfather's stories, the ones his brother loves to pry out of the man. Tales of thwarting escapes from the first days of the wall. Arresting traitors. Making East Berlin safe from Western influence. Lothar Muller, hero of the socialist state.

His grandfather laughs without mirth. His voice is as cold as this barren room. Kurt flashes to the time he met Lina's grandfather, a kindly old man who scooped her up in his arms and took them out for ice cream and a walk in the park to feed the ducks. That was what grandparents were supposed to be like! Lothar Muller has always been a stranger.

"The Stasi is East Berlin itself," he says. "Much bigger than any one person. And it swallowed me up years ago. If things were different, I might be able to provide you safer passage to the West. Forged papers, most likely. But I am not trusted. I haven't been for a very long time. My access is very limited. If I were to involve anyone else in this—a forger, a border guard—we would all be caught. And trying to drive you across the border would be futile. I might as well drive us straight to Hohenschönhausen."

Kurt shivers again at the mention of the infamous Stasi prison.

"Do you understand why I'm telling you this?"

Kurt imagines a vast chessboard, pieces moving far beyond reason or logic. "I don't really understand why you do anything."

At this, his grandfather laughs with more genuine feeling than Kurt's ever heard from the man. "Because I love you, and I want the best for you."

In an evening full of strange and astonishing things, this beats them all. Kurt is speechless. *Love?* From Lothar Muller? A man who's never shown the slightest interest in his life until now? A man who doesn't seem to care that his own son has been permanently exiled to the West?

"Um," Kurt says, "I love you too?"

"No, you don't." He says this so matter-of-factly, Kurt doesn't even put up a false protest. "So," Lothar continues. "You have three days until they suspend schiessbefehl for the Swedish prime minister's visit, and then we make our move."

Kurt thinks of the view from the chess academy window. The garden plots, the hinterland wall, the death strip. "In Treptow?" he says.

His grandfather radiates displeasure. "You mean, the very place you talked about crossing on the recordings from your living room? No, Kurt. I'm afraid that won't do."

"Oh," Kurt says. "Right."

"You will cross in the exact place I tell you, at the exact time. I will take care of the rest. And after tonight, there's no going back. No calling it off. Once I set this plan in motion, it will proceed of its own accord. And it will be too dangerous to contact me again. You *must* go through with it. Do you hear me? Otherwise it will fall apart."

"Yes."

"Then you only have to do one more thing."

"What's that?"

"Practice climbing."

"Did your grandfather really say it was okay to take me with you?" Lina asks.

At her side, Kurt holds the nylon rope in his hands. The metal hook dangles by his knees. The excess rope coils at his feet. He looks up at the old brick wall that rises from dense foliage. Outlined against the evening sky, it looks like the battlements of some remote Scottish castle. It had once been part of a massive storage building at the edge of the Johannisthal Airfield in the middle of Adlershof. Now it's a crumbling ruin, even more neglected than the hotel where he met his grandfather last night. Except for some furtive takeoffs and landings that everybody knows are Soviet planes, nobody's used the airfield since before he was born.

"He didn't exactly say I *couldn't*," Kurt says. "So, do I just sort of . . . toss this thing up there?"

"Underhanded," Lina says. "Give it a few big twirls first."

Kurt hesitates. "How many twirls?"

"I don't know, three?"

Kurt rotates his wrist to get the hook swinging, then moves his forearm to give it momentum. The metal hook slices through the air with a *whoosh*. He leans to his left so it doesn't accidentally smack him in the head. On the third rotation he opens his hand. The hook flies up toward the top of the wall—and stops halfway with a sudden tug. Then it falls down into the bushes.

"You're stepping on the rope," Lina points out.

"Oops." Kurt moves his foot. "That's what Frau Petrovsky would call a self-checkmate."

He reels in the hook, dragging a clump of dead leaves, and begins to coil the rope in his left hand.

Lina grinds the toe of her shoe into the earth. "So you didn't actually ask him."

"I didn't get a chance to. He's not like your grandpa. He's kind of . . . prickly."

"Well, it doesn't matter. I'm still not going with you, and I'm still mad that you're going. The only reason I'm even helping you practice is because I don't want you to fall off the top of the wall and break your head."

"I'm not going to break my head." With the rope coiled loosely in his left hand, he uses his right to twirl the hook. *One, two, three!*

He lets it fly. The hook clinks against the wall and falls into the underbrush, scraping the bricks on the way down.

He turns to Lina. In what scant daylight remains, she's a girl from a black-and-white movie. He can barely make out her face, but he can sense her nerves.

"I'll get it eventually," he says. "Don't worry."

"Don't tell me not to worry." She gives his shoulder a little shove. "Don't do this, Kurt. Seriously. Just don't."

"I have to. My grandfather says it's in motion. He says there's no backing out now."

"He's *Stasi*, Kurt. Plus he's your stupid brother's hero—that should tell you everything you know about whether you can trust him."

"I don't know." Kurt reels in the hook. "He seems sad."

Lina coughs. "He seems *sad*? He's spent his entire life wearing disguises and spying on people and tricking them into doing things. Don't you think it would be pretty easy for him to trick *you*?"

"He found the bugs in the living room."

"That could have been part of the trick. To get you to trust him. That and his sad act."

Kurt looks up at the top of the wall. He visualizes the grappling hook clearing the top row of bricks, the metal spikes catching and holding fast. It's just like chess, he tells himself. See the next move. Watch it happen in your mind. Then make it happen.

He spins the hook and lets it fly.

It sails up into the air. The rope uncoils without a hitch. There's a *snikt* as the hook catches atop the wall. He gives the line a tug. It stays taut and doesn't give way.

"See?" He turns to Lina, triumphant. "I'm the greatest climber in Berlin."

"We're not gonna have this anymore when you're gone," she says as he stomps down some of the brush to get closer to the base of the wall.

"What do you mean, *this*?" He grips the rope with both hands and places one foot against the wall. He leans in. The nubs on the climbing shoes—which fit perfectly—find purchase against the brick. He hoists himself up and places two feet against the wall.

"*This*. What we're doing right now. Just hanging out together," Lina says. "Besides just playing chess, I mean. Think of all the stuff teenagers get to do. That'll be us pretty soon. We can actually go places together."

"They don't let you go places in East Germany."

"That's not true!" she protests. "We could go to Poland someday! Or Latvia! Or Russia! Anyway, that's not the point. The point is, once you cross over, they're not just going to let you come back to visit. Or even call."

"I know that, but . . ." A feeling he doesn't entirely understand wells up. "Stop distracting me, okay?" He works his way up, hand over hand, one vertical "step" at a time. His heart pounds as he ascends. He knows he's not supposed to look down, but in his mind the ground is a whole kilometer below, with Lina no bigger than a speck of dust. The last of the dying light has vanished now, and the top of the wall is a blank space offset by the night's first stars.

He has climbed all the way into the stratosphere. The air is thin. And there's no one to hear you scream in the vacuum of space.

"Why did you stop?" she says.

"What?" Kurt's head clears. He's only climbed halfway up—about six feet off the ground. "Oh. This is kind of hard!" He gathers himself for the rest of the climb.

"Maybe you should stick to chess. Maybe climbing isn't really your thing."

"Watch this!"

To show her, he resumes his climb, moving faster and faster, ignoring the mounting ache in his upper arms. After all, he'll have to move quickly on the night of the actual escape. There's no sense practicing climbing slowly. Despite the strain, he can't help but smile to himself as he reaches the top—if Franz could see him now. The discipline! The strength!

At the top of the wall, he peers out across the vast expanse of the airfield. Lights from the single working runway are a distant line of white dots in the night.

"It's colder up here!" he calls back down to Lina.

"It is not!"

"Yes, it is! Because of the elevation!"

"Would you just come back down?"

He takes one more look out across the airfield, imagining the view from atop the hinterland wall. Signal fence, tank traps, supply road, death strip, outer wall. So much ground to cover. His stomach clenches. He tries to dismiss the thought, but the real wall is waiting for him, and there's nothing he can do to change that now.

"Coming."

The moment he begins his descent, his arms start to burn again. He grits his teeth and imagines Franz screaming insults at him as his strength ebbs away. He reaches the bottom, plants his feet in the underbrush, and lets go of the rope.

"Too slow," Lina says.

He takes a moment to catch his breath. "It was my first try."

"So what do you think?"

"About what?"

"About what I said. About it being the end of all this if you make it to the West."

"Lina, would you stop? It doesn't have to be the end of anything. Just come with me."

"I told you, my parents are here."

"Well, my parents are there! And at least your parents are nice. I have to live with Franz."

"So come live with us downstairs."

Kurt stretches an arm behind his head. "Did your parents say I could do that?"

"They didn't exactly say you couldn't."

For a little while, neither one of them says anything. A strange feeling settles over him—like they're having this discussion just to hear it out loud. That both of them know it isn't going to change anything.

Lina breaks the silence. "I have something for you." She rummages inside her handbag and comes up with what appears to be a large remote control for a TV. When she hands it to him, Kurt still can't tell what it is. Lina reaches over, presses a button, and a small screen lights up. English words parade across. Then a familiar board appears. And little pixelated chess pieces.

"An electronic chess game?" Kurt has heard of these but never seen one. And certainly never imagined he'd actually get to *play* one. "It must be from America—how did you get this?"

"I have my ways," she says.

Kurt knows she must have found it on the black market, likely through an older kid at school, and traded some prized possession for it. "Thank you. It's amazing."

"You can pretend the computer is me," she says. "Which shouldn't be too hard, since it'll probably beat you every time."

"I don't know what to say," Kurt mutters.

"Say you won't go."

He doesn't want to lie—not to Lina, not now. So he doesn't say anything at all, just sits down in the tall grass and presses start to begin the game. Lina sits down next to him, and for the first time ever, they play chess together on the same side.

Kurt dreams of bugs. Listening devices sprouting wires like legs bristling with little hairs. Microphones as fuzzy mandibles. Thorax batteries in squishy segments. Abdomens of cathodes, eyes of dials. Hundreds of them crawling in the walls, nesting in the television, swarming from radio speakers.

Even now, seated at the table with his brother in what he knows to be his waking life, the whole apartment seethes with the sounds of skittering insects. A tireless colony that's always listening.

This whole place makes him itch. He's become allergic to the apartment itself.

On TV, the newscaster on the state program *Aktuelle Kamera* drones on about Poland and something called "Solidarity."

Kurt isn't paying any attention. Poland is farther east, and after tomorrow night, the East will no longer interest him in the slightest. A harsh burst of static interrupts the broadcast. Across the table, Franz tosses down his fork, gets out of his chair, and brings his fist down hard on top of the television. Clarity returns.

Bugs, Kurt thinks. *Bugs in the TV, squirming around, messing up the signal.*

"They think they can just form their own labor unions now," his brother says.

"Who, the bugs?" Kurt bends to his sauerbraten and cuts it into little pieces.

"What? No, these Polish upstarts," he says. "These Solidarity fools. They're ungrateful."

"Uh-huh," Kurt says.

"Hey!" Franz snaps his fingers. "Chuckles! How's the food?"

"It's really good," Kurt says. "And I don't even like sauerbraten that much."

Franz laughs. "What kind of German doesn't like sauerbraten?" He forks up a huge bite of gravy-soaked beef.

"I'm thinking of becoming a vegetarian."

Franz glares as he chews. "This better not be some kind of punk thing."

"I don't want to get meat gravy on my black-market Levi's and leather jacket, you know?" *Bugs,* he thinks, glancing over at the radio. *Bugs, bugs, bugs.* "I'm just joking," he adds, for the benefit of the unseen listeners.

"My brother, the comedian." Franz mops up gravy with a fluffy dinner roll, pops it into his mouth, and sits back in his chair. "Seriously, how are you, Kurt?"

"Um," Kurt says. "What?"

Franz gives him an oddly gentle smile. "How are you doing? You never tell me what's going on with you. How's chess going?"

"Oh. Good."

"*Oh.*" Franz imitates his deadpan voice. "*Good.* That's all you have to say?"

Kurt shrugs. "It's fine."

"Good *and* fine. Now we're making some real progress." Franz picks up his fork and uses it to point at Kurt. "Something's up with you."

Kurt's heart beats faster. "Nothing's up. I'm just tired. I haven't been sleeping well."

"What's on your mind?" Franz sets the fork down. "You can talk to me. I'd like to know what's going on with you. We're not roommates. I'm your brother."

There's an uncomfortable echo of their grandfather in his brother's words. Some kind of emotional overlap Kurt can't quite put his finger on. Professions of love, and of interest in his life—but Kurt has the feeling that love is something built carefully over time, not something tossed out like bait in the water.

"There's a lot going on, actually," he says.

"Like what?"

"Just stuff."

"All right, Kurt. If you won't share anything with me, I'll share something with you. We received some good news today."

We meaning: the grepos, the trapos, the army, the government. All of the above, perhaps.

Kurt scoops up some red cabbage.

"The Swedish prime minister came down with a bad flu," his brother says. "His trip is canceled."

Kurt's heart races. He tries to keep his hand steady as he lifts the cabbage to his mouth. Suddenly, it has no taste. "Oh," he manages to say. "I hope he feels better soon."

His brother gives him a strange look. "Yes, let us join hands and wish him a swift recovery. In the meantime, since he won't be here meeting with Honecker, there will be no suspension of schiessbefehl tomorrow night. It's business as usual up on the wall."

Kurt's teeth churn methodically, mashing up his tasteless cabbage. His brother is staring right at him. He takes a sip of water. The sip turns into a gulp. He drains his glass and sets it down. He imagines a room full of Stasi goons with earpieces in, waiting for him to say something.

But all he can think of is the grappling hook, and how long it's going to take him to scale the hinterland wall. Now he has to do it knowing that the shoot-to-kill order is back on. So he'll be making his way up the wall, through the signal fence, and across the death strip with a target on his back.

He swallows. "That's good," he says.

Franz cocks his head. This clearly wasn't the response he was anticipating. "I'm glad you approve."

"Of course I approve. A nation must defend its walls."

Franz considers this. Then his expression darkens. "I truly hope that one day you'll see that guarding against spies from the West and traitors from within is no laughing matter."

"I'm not laughing!" Kurt protests. He's in the swing of it now. He believes he's actually starting to sound sincere. "You always think I'm making fun of you, but I'm not. I'm *glad* you're out there protecting us. How could you do it properly without schiessbefehl?"

"Right," his brother says. A note of lingering suspicion floats across the table. "How could we?"

"So," Kurt says, "what's this Solidarity thing they're talking about?"

As his brother launches into an impassioned speech about a bunch of Polish shipbuilders who became puppets of the Americans, Kurt's mind wanders ahead to tomorrow night. The rest of the meal passes in a nervous blur as he goes over the plan in his mind.

Over the hinterland wall with the grappling hook. Through a service opening in the signal fence—its alarm and shock sensors disabled by his grandfather, dressed as a grepo commander. Carefully past the tank traps and across the supply road, the ditch, and the death strip while his grandfather keeps the guards in the tower occupied. Then over the outer wall with a ladder stashed ahead of time by Lothar. (This wall, with its cemented pipe along the top, is made to repel grappling hooks.)

He imagines all of it through the eyes of a grepo like Franz, lining Kurt up in the sight of his rifle, following him as he moves across the death strip, pulling the trigger as he struggles with the ladder, or stumbles into the ditch, or gets tripped up in a million other ways.

His back tingles, right between his shoulder blades. His brother wraps up his speech.

"Wow," Kurt says for the benefit of the bugs. Under the table, his leg bounces furiously. He feels like he's going to be sick. "Solidarity. They ought to be shot."

T he night of January 31 is clear and mild. Kurt wishes the full moon would go hide behind a cloud. With his brother at work, he stands at the window for a long time, urging the sky to cooperate.

Frau Petrovsky once told the class about the famous 1972 chess match between the American Bobby Fischer and the Soviet champion Boris Spassky (who opened, Kurt recalls, with Nimzo-Indian). Fischer started poorly, and it wasn't until the television cameras were taken away and the game moved to a private room that the American turned things around and won the match.

Fischer had the right idea, Kurt thinks. When you're dealing with the might of a brutal state, you have to be sneaky about things. You have to make your moves in the dark. Beat them at their own game.

He gives the bright moon the stink eye. Then he takes his time loading a few meager possessions into the backpack his grandfather gave him: climbing shoes, grappling hook, a single change of clothes, the portable chess game from Lina. Plus some extra batteries he found in a cupboard.

He puts on a coat that's too light for winter. He doesn't want to climb and run in his heavy jacket. At the door he gives his apartment one last look. He tells himself he won't miss it, but he still feels a pang as he steps out into the corridor.

Before dawn he'll be in Kreuzberg, he tells himself. And once he's in his parents' apartment, he'll forget all about this place. He heads down the stairs, past Lina's door. He remembers the first time they ever played together, when they were six years old. She'd been so obsessed with one of his toy trucks that he'd let her take it home.

Between the truck and the chess game, their gift giving has come full circle.

Outside the front door, he zips his coat and stands with his hands in his pockets, surveying the mostly empty street. The closest streetlight is broken, and the pale glow cast down from the moon plays along the cracked pavement. He takes one last look up to his apartment window, then heads down the sidewalk toward the S-Bahn station at Johannisthal.

"Pssst! Hey, kid!"

The voice comes out of the shadows, underneath the eaves of a boarded-up corner store. He picks up the pace.

Footsteps fall in behind him. His heart begins to hammer.

A hand comes down on his shoulder. He whirls around, ready to give his assailant a shove and run for it—only to find Lina about to break into laughter.

A warm rush overtakes him and he wraps her up in a hug. His hands brush the backpack slung across her shoulder. He holds her at arm's length and looks her in the eyes. "Are you coming with me?"

She shrugs. "Somebody's gotta make sure you don't break your head."

21

The stretch of the Berlin Wall that bulges from Mitte in the east to Kreuzberg in the west looks like any other. Kurt and Lina study it from across the street, huddled together by a well-kept shrub on the grounds of Sankt-Michael-Kirche. The hinterland wall rises cold and implacable against the night sky. Kurt can't see beyond it, but he knows exactly what's waiting for him on the other side.

He can only a hope a ladder is one of those things. Along with a disarmed signal fence.

He points up Engeldamm, the road that runs along the base of the wall. Three blocks away, an observation tower rises. "My grandfather should be in there right now. Taking charge of the grepos. Clearing a path for us."

"We have no way of knowing," Lina points out.

"We just have to trust him. And then once we're over the wall, we never have to think about who to trust, and who's an informer, ever again. Things don't work like that in the West."

She stands up and shoulders her backpack. "I guess we'll find out."

"Hey, Lina." She turns. "I'm glad you're here."

"Me too."

Sheltered by the churchyard, he retrieves the grappling hook from his backpack. "As soon as we hit the wall, I'm throwing it up there," Kurt says. He straightens up, takes a deep breath, and gives Lina a nod. "Let's do this."

They run across the road. He grips the coiled nylon tightly in his fists. The weight of the metal hook is comforting somehow. He can feel the potential energy building in his arm, waiting to be unleashed as he flings the hook over the top of the hinterland wall. They're really going to do it!

Checkmate, Franz. Checkmate, Honecker. Checkmate, East Berlin.

Suddenly, a car whips around the bend, tires squealing, and tears up Engeldamm, bearing down on them. Kurt freezes in his tracks. Lina takes him by the sleeve of his coat and pulls him across the road, out of the way.

The car comes to a shrieking halt right beside them.

A black Opel, Kurt thinks. *Stasi.* He drops the grappling hook and grabs Lina's hand. They hold each other tightly. Despair swamps him—*so close.*

The window rolls down. A middle-aged grepo leans out. "Get in, you fool!"

A surge of relief nearly brings him to his knees. "Grandfather?" Kurt peers at the man's bushy salt-and-pepper mustache, his heavy jowls. "What are you doing here?"

"I said *in!*"

Kurt opens the rear door and steps aside to let Lina in first.

"Not her," his grandfather says. "Just you. Hurry! There isn't time."

"She's coming with me," Kurt says.

"I can't get two of you across," he says. "It's you alone, or nothing. Make up your mind. This car's leaving in ten seconds."

Lina shoves him through the door. "Go! I'll see you again."

"Wait, how? When?"

She turns her back without another word and runs off into the night.

Kurt fights the urge to follow her, to convince her to come back, to convince his grandfather that both of them have to get to West Berlin. Instead, he shuts the door. There's a neat pile of clothes on the seat beside him.

His grandfather pulls a U-turn and heads up Engeldamm toward the guard tower.

"What's going on?" Kurt says. "This isn't the plan."

"The prime minister canceled his visit. Franz informed you of this. Schiessbefehl is active. Yet still you proceeded?"

"You told me I had to! That everything was already in motion!"

"They would have shot you! You're just like your parents. No instinct for self-preservation. Now put those on."

Kurt reaches for the folded clothes. His heart sinks. It's a pair of trousers, a white collared shirt, a red necktie. The uniform of the Young Pioneers.

"You have got to be kidding me."

"The plan has changed. Clearly."

His grandfather takes a sharp left at Heinrich-Heine-Strasse. The city comes alive in a blur of streetlights and activity. A few blocks up the road, the lights illuminate shiny slats of corrugated metal huts. Between them, a red-and-white-striped barrier extends across the narrow road. Beyond this is a miniature labyrinth of "slalom fencing"—a lane that zigzags back and forth to prevent anyone from crashing straight through. Outside the two guard huts, four armed grepos are milling about.

Kurt's heart is in his throat. "I thought you said we couldn't go through a checkpoint."

The car slows down. "We're not. You are. Now *get changed*. Throw your old clothes and your backpack out the window. You take nothing with you."

Kurt does as he's told, scrambling to undress and change in the cramped back seat. The awful uniform fits him perfectly, of course. He stuffs his old clothes into the bag and his grandfather pulls to the side of the street so he can toss it out. At the last moment, Kurt pulls the chess game from the bag. Then he rolls down the window and drops the bag into the gutter.

His grandfather makes straight for the checkpoint. "Follow my lead. When things go bad, run. Stay low, keep your head down. No matter what you hear, keep going. Don't stop. Don't turn around."

"What do you mean *go bad*? What's going to happen to you when I run?"

"Let me worry about that."

"No," Kurt says. "Let's just call it off and go home."

"You are going to West Berlin," his grandfather says fiercely. "Tonight. You are going to tell your father that I love him, and that I'm sorry I couldn't do more. You are going to grow up and pursue whatever makes you happy."

They pull up to the checkpoint. A young grepo comes jogging over. Lothar rolls down the window.

"Papers, please," the grepo says without even bothering to look inside. He sounds very bored. He holds out his hand.

"Your uniform is wrinkled," Lothar says. "And half your shirt is untucked."

The grepo peers into the open window. Then he straightens up and stands at attention. "Herr Oberst!"

"Open the gate."

The grepo hesitates. "Sir?"

"Inspection."

"There's nothing scheduled." Now he glances into the back of the car and makes eye contact with Kurt and looks very confused.

"That's the point of an inspection," Lothar says. "I gave you an order."

"Right." He nods smartly and scurries off. Kurt marvels at the way his grandfather forced his will on the poor grepo in a matter of seconds. He jams the chess game into his trouser pocket. It barely fits and pulls the fabric tight against his thigh. Plus it looks ridiculous, this rectangular bulge against his hip.

The striped barrier lifts. The Opel surges forward through the first gate.

Suddenly, a second grepo steps in front of the car and waves his arms above his head. Kurt's grandfather doesn't stop, and for a split second Kurt thinks he's going to run the man down. A quick glance to the side reveals the first grepo standing by the barrier, his hand resting on his sidearm. His grandfather hits the brakes. The second grepo approaches the window but keeps his distance.

"I must ask you to step out and show me your papers, please."

"Stand aside, *Leutnant,*" Lothar replies.

"Herr Oberst, with respect, this is highly irregular. Who is the boy in the back seat?"

"The contest winner." He says this like the grepo is a complete idiot for not knowing about the contest. "The Young Pioneer who scored the best on our History of the Republic quiz gets to tour every checkpoint in a single night. Heinrich-Heine-Strasse is next on our list."

"I was not informed."

"I am informing you now."

This second grepo isn't as cowed by Lothar's manner. "I'm going to have to phone this in. In the meantime, please step out of the car and show me your papers. Both of you."

Kurt slides toward the door but freezes when he sees that Lothar hasn't moved at all. "Your commanding officer is going to hear about this, I assure you."

"I am sorry, Herr Oberst, but you know our protocol better than anyone. Without proper authorization, no one gets through."

Lothar rolls up the window and turns to look at Kurt. "Get ready."

He opens the door, takes his cane from the front seat, and steps out. Kurt joins him a moment later. His earlier worries about the full moon seem silly now that he's being blasted by floodlights. The grepos huddle to talk things over. After a while, one of them goes inside the silver hut. Kurt's grandfather stands ramrod straight, jabbing his cane into the pavement like he wants to stab it straight down into the ground.

A strange sort of calm settles over Kurt. There will be time, once he's safely over the border, to sort out all the chaos in his mind. He breathes in and out, in and out.

The leutnant emerges from the hut. He's trailed by a third grepo.

"There's no record of any such contest!" the third man calls out almost gleefully. "You're going to have to come with us."

Kurt gasps. He'd recognize that voice anywhere. He turns to his grandfather. *"Franz!"*

His brother crosses the lane in three steps and stops short. "Kurt?" Then he studies the "grepo commander" at his side. "Grandfather?"

To his brother's credit, Franz looks utterly shocked for only a split second before he regains his composure. "What's going on here? What's this about a contest?"

"Franz," his grandfather says. For the first time, his icy tone begins to crack. Kurt realizes that he is as surprised as any of them. "You must get out of here. Now."

Franz looks confused. "I can't leave my post." He looks from Lothar to Kurt. "What is this?" The wrongness of it seems to dawn on him all at once. "What's happening?"

Lothar Muller heaves a great sigh. Then he turns to Kurt. "Go," he says softly.

The leutnant reaches for his holstered pistol. With astonishing quickness, Lothar brings up his heavy wooden cane and cracks the man across the face, sending him reeling.

Someone inside the hut hits the button to lower the gate. Kurt takes off and barely ducks beneath it before it comes down like a blade. Behind him, he hears his brother scream *"STOP,"* but whether it's directed at him or his grandfather he does not know.

On the other side of the gate is the first sharp turn of the slalom fences. Kurt takes it so fast he stumbles and nearly crashes to the pavement. His arms windmill, his hip slams against a pile of sandbags, and he rights himself. He feels like he's ice skating.

His brother cries out, *"Don't shoot!"*

Again, Kurt has no idea if he means *don't shoot at the fleeing boy* or *don't shoot at the old man.* He just keeps running.

The other grepos ignore his brother's plea. The first shot splits the night. A sandbag off to his right explodes in a cloudburst of fine-grained mist. A guttural cry escapes him. His fear reaches a new place, beyond anything he's ever known. His whole body tingles. His feet are weightless in their climbing shoes as they skim the concrete.

More floodlights come on. An alarm blares. The checkpoint is as bright as a summer's day. He rounds another sharp turn, folding himself up like an American football player on the run, trying to keep his head lower than the top of the sandbags.

There's another *crack*. This time, the bullet pings off the fence next to his ear and there's a sharp stinging pain and a searing heat along the side of his head.

Still alive, he thinks. *Just a graze.*

More shouting at his back. He can't pick out his brother's voice anymore. Or his grandfather's.

He rounds another corner. There is commotion up ahead—uniformed officers behind another gate. Two of them kneel and take aim with their rifles. At first he despairs, and almost stops to put his hands up, but then he realizes they're not yelling at him to stop; they're urging him onward. And the weapons aren't pointed at him—they're trained on the opposite side of the checkpoint.

This is the West German border guard.

Just a few more meters and he'll be in Kreuzberg. He sprints toward the gate as it lifts to welcome him to West Berlin.

A final shot echoes across the checkpoint. One of the voices at his back falls silent. He stumbles and hits the ground as he crosses the official borderline. The chess game digs into his leg. He rolls over and wriggles it out of his pocket.

A West German guard rushes over to help him to his feet. Kurt presses a button on the game. The screen comes to life. The words scroll. The board appears. Gasping for breath, he holds it up to show the first person he's ever spoken to on West German soil.

"It still works!"

EPILOGUE

The man in the denim jacket is not used to handling a sledgehammer. Marta Dietrich can tell by the way he hefts it awkwardly over his shoulder like a little kid with a baseball bat. When he swings it, the impact takes a chunk of spray-painted concrete out of the side of the wall. The crowd presses in, the fury on their faces aimed straight at the wall itself. They delight in its destruction.

It is nearly midnight, and it looks as if all of Berlin has gathered at the edge of Unter den Linden in the shadow of the Brandenburg Gate.

The Western news broadcasts are saying that the borders are open. After twenty-eight years, the wall has fallen.

What are the Eastern broadcasts saying? It doesn't matter. No one is listening to them anyway.

The grepos seem confused and lost. No one lifts a hand to stop people crossing back and forth through checkpoints and over railway bridges. Marta has seen East Berliners race one another, laughing and shouting, across the death strips. She has been one of them, going back and forth, West to East and back again, with no purpose in mind other than the freedom of the crossing itself.

The only danger now is getting sprayed with champagne.

Marta works her way through the ecstatic throng until she's nearly pressed up against the wall on the Western side. History is every moment that's passed, she thinks. Most of them simply gone. Surely not every event that becomes famous feels like history at the time of its unfolding. But there is no doubt that this moment does. What else could it be?

The wall has a flat top here, just beyond the Pariser Platz and the magnificent gate itself. There are hundreds of people standing on it and sitting with their legs dangling. Some hold hands. Some just stare off into the distance. The sledgehammer cracks again and again.

Suddenly, an arm reaches down in front of her face.

"Need a lift?"

Marta looks up. The arm is attached to a boy of twelve or thirteen. He's dressed in a leather jacket. There are pins in the shape of chess pieces stuck to the lapel. His hair is gelled into tall spikes, dyed neon purple. He smiles.

"Sure," Marta says. She reaches up and takes his hand. Someone in the crowd, without being asked, helps by hoisting her feet. She laughs as she's lifted into the air. A moment later, she finds herself atop the wall. She can feel the sledgehammer blows vibrate up through her feet.

"Thank you," she says. "So, what do you make of all this?"

"It's incredible," he says. "I've only been in West Berlin since January."

Marta smiles. "You know, it's funny, I was right around your age when I came over too."

"How did you do it?"

"I took a train. How about you?"

"My grandfather helped me."

"Sounds like a good man."

The boy considers this for a moment. "I think he tried to be."

"Is he here with you now?"

The boy shakes his head. His purple spikes waggle. "He didn't make it. I found out later." He pauses. "They shot him."

"I'm sorry," Marta says. "I'll make a line for him."

"What do you mean?"

"It's something my father used to do that I inherited. A line on a chalkboard for each person killed trying to get over the wall."

"Huh. Now that the wall's coming down, maybe you can erase it."

Marta thinks of line number eight. The brother she never got to see grow up. "I don't know."

The boy reaches into his pocket and pulls out a chunk of concrete. One side is smooth and covered in yellow paint. "That guy smashing up the wall gave me this. You want it?"

Marta is surprised to find that she does. "Thank you."

He lifts the headphones draped around his neck and places them over his ears. "All right, well, I'm going to keep looking for my friend. I'm Kurt, by the way."

They shake hands. "Marta."

"Nice to meet you." He turns to head deeper into the crowd.

"Hey, Kurt!" Marta calls after him. She cups her hands around her mouth. "Welcome to Germany!"

AUTHOR'S NOTE

During my research into both the first and final days of the Berlin Wall, I came across more incredible stories of personal heroism, courage, and sacrifice by German citizens in both East and West (and in the tunnels and sewers connecting them) than could possibly fit into one book. I have tried to pay tribute to a few of these stories by drawing inspiration from them for various characters and events. The extended Dietrich family is based on the Deterling family, who really did commandeer a train for a cinematic escape to West Berlin. In 1961, Harry Deterling drove a speeding steam-powered locomotive through the Albrechtshof station and across the border with thirty-two people aboard, including many family members. Amazingly, several of his passengers had simply boarded the train, only to find themselves part of an escape plan they hadn't known about. Upon reaching the West, seven of them turned around and went back to the East.

The Deterlings' story, along with many other daring and often doomed escape attempts, are detailed in Frederick Taylor's excellent book *The Berlin Wall*, a comprehensive account of the circumstances surrounding the rise, growth, and eventual fall of the "Anti-Fascist Protection Barrier," as the East German authorities labeled it with their typical flair for the sinister and the bureaucratic. Some details of Kurt's abandoned grappling hook plan and Stefan and Johann's swim across Humboldt Harbor come from this book, along with a wealth of other information on daily life in East Berlin, including the old communist joke, "we pretend to work and they pretend to pay us."

I relied on Anna Funder's *Stasiland* to bring the character of Lothar Muller to life and to give the activities of the secret police an air of authenticity. (The signals Muller teaches his class, for example, are part of the actual Stasi surveillance tactics.) At its peak the Stasi employed 97,000 people and relied on the eyes and ears of 173,000 informers. It's no wonder that in East Berlin, the smallest interactions with friends, neighbors, and classmates could be cause for paranoia and mistrust. Muller's troubling revelation that most ordinary people choose to inform for almost nothing in return is one of the many insights taken from this lively yet melancholy book.

I would also like to cite John le Carré's classic novel *The Spy Who Came In from the Cold*, from which I took both black Opel cars and the notion of the ends justifying the means in the espionage game. Maxim Leo's *Red Love* helped fill in some gaps in the day-to-day lives of the characters, and Mary Elise Sarotte's *The Collapse* provided details on the wall's final days, hours, and minutes. I would recommend all these books to anyone interested in learning more about the true story of the Berlin Wall and life in East Berlin.

Real historical figures haunt the margins of this novel, though few make any appearances on the page. One exception to this is Karl-Eduard von Schnitzler, the face and voice of *Der Schwarze Kanal—The Black Channel*. This propaganda broadcast aired on East German TV for the entire existence of the Berlin Wall. Though von Schnitzler's monologues in this book are fictional, I based them on real statements, including bits and pieces of his fascinating interview in *Stasiland*. Similarly, the passage from *Neues Deutschland* that follows the prologue of this book was inspired by excerpts from that paper reprinted in Frederick Taylor's *The Berlin Wall*.

Without the authors and works mentioned above, this book would not exist. Any historical inaccuracies, geographical impossibilities, and tweaks to time and space should be blamed on me and me alone.

ABOUT THE AUTHOR

Andy Marino is the author of *Escape from Chernobyl*, the Plot to Kill Hitler trilogy, and several other novels for young readers. He lives in upstate New York with his partner and their dog. You can visit him at andy-marino.com.